PRAISE FOR THE NOVELS OF
KATIE MacALISTER

Memoirs of a Dragon Hunter
"Bursting with the author's trademark zany humor and spicy romance . . . this quick tale will delight paranormal romance fans."—*Publishers Weekly*

Sparks Fly
"Balanced by a well-organized plot and MacAlister's trademark humor."—*Publishers Weekly*

It's All Greek to Me
"A fun and sexy read."—*The Season for Romance*
"A wonderful lighthearted romantic romp as a kick-butt American Amazon and a hunky Greek find love. Filled with humor, fans will laugh with the zaniness of Harry meets Yacky."—*Midwest Book Review*

Much Ado About Vampires
"A humorous take on the dark and demonic."—*USA Today*
"Once again this author has done a wonderful job. I was sucked into the world of Dark Ones right from the start and was taken on a fantastic ride. This book is full of witty dialogue and great romance, making it one that should not be missed."—Fresh Fiction

The Unbearable Lightness of Dragons
"Had me laughing out loud. . . . This book is full of humor and romance, keeping the reader entertained all the way through . . . a wondrous story full of magic. . . . I cannot wait to see what happens next in the lives of the dragons."—Fresh Fiction

YOU SLEIGH ME

A NOVELLA OF THE OTHERWORLD

KATIE MACALISTER

FAT CAT BOOKS

Cover by Croco Designs
Formatting by Racing Pigeon Productions

This book is for everyone who for years (and I mean YEARS) badgered...er...requested that I write a book with both dragons and vampires. You're the bestest!

STELLA PENDLETON NOTES

Date: 23 December
Location: Ontario

Significant individuals encountered:

Drake Vireo, wyvern of green dragons. Handsome as the day is long, but too interested in his mate to be any fun.

Aisling Grey, mate of above. Also a demon lord and Guardian. How did she end up that way? Inquiring minds want to know.

Effrijim, demon in Newfoundland dog form. Annoying. Might be troublesome in the future.

Gabriel Tauhou, wyvern of silver dragons. Also handsome, with bonus dimples.

May Northcott, mate of Gabriel. Tetchy. Is a doppelganger. I never did trust those.

Kostya Fekete, wyvern of black dragons. Argumentative and prone to sulks. Handsome, though. What is it about the dragons? Do they all look like models? Are there any ugly ones?

Baltic (no last name mentioned), wyvern of light dragons. Son of demigod dragon progenitor. Watchful.

Intense. Broods well, though. Wouldn't kick him out of bed for eating crackers. Don't trust him farther than I could swing a behemoth, though.

Ysolde, mate of Baltic. Sassy and irreverent. Caught her looking at me oddly a few times.

Brom, son of Ysolde. Typical male of young years, introspective and wholly self-absorbed.

Christian Dante, Dark One. Head of Moravian Council. Distracted by the presence of dragons, and defensive of his Beloved.

Allie, Beloved of Christian. Fairly easygoing. Not overly astute, I think. Very, very wrong about some things.

Finch Dante, Dark One. Quiet and apparently bound up in his own problems.

Karma Marx, poltergeist. Works for Akashic League. Doesn't appear to be very aware about beings in the Otherworld.

Adam Dirgesinger, poltergeist. Also works for Akashic League and some mortal police force. Apparently romantically bound to Karma. Quiet, but watchful.

Pixie O'Hara, poltergeist. Teenager. Enough said.

HOUR ONE
AISLING

"You can bite my shiny pink tinsel-covered ass."

"Jim!" I spun around to apologize to the red dragon who had helped unload the last of our luggage, but given the rate the snow was falling, he'd already leaped into the car and was speeding off as quickly as he could.

"What?" my furry demon in dog form asked, blinking in surprise.

I grabbed it by its festive red collar, and leaned down to say in a voice that I hope dripped with threat, "That is not only *not* a nice thing to say to the driver just because he turned on the car radio, but the very fact that you are speaking out in the open where mortals can hear you is way out of line. If you can't keep your lips zipped until we get on the plane, then I'll be happy to command you to silence."

"István started it," Jim said, its eyes wide with feigned innocence. "He's trying to make me lose Whamageddon by paying everyone to turn on radios around me, and hiding my headphones so I have to hear the music."

"István?" A shape hove up next to me in the flurry of snow, resolving itself into that of a woman slightly shorter than me, with brown, shoulder-length hair cut in a bob, and a pair of glasses that was quickly spotted with melting snow. Stella Pendleton had met us about an hour ago, when we picked her up at a train station.

"István is one of Drake's bodyguards," I told her. "He left early this morning to go on a holiday vacation with his girlfriend. Which is well and fine, except Pal—that's Drake's other bodyguard—is in England with my mentor Nora, who is his significant other, which leaves us stuck with the mountain of luggage that Drake deems necessary for an emergency three-day visit to Canada. What on earth is Whamageddon?"

"Sheesh," Jim said, moseying past me, "I would hate to be so old that I was downright clueless."

"You are more than a thousand years older than me, buster," I said, but remembered in time where we were, and cut short my lecture.

I glanced around to make sure no one else heard us. Luckily, with the crappy weather and incoming blizzard, the small airport in what Jim had referred to as the armpit of Ontario had limited the number of holiday travelers, and the drop-off zone was empty of everyone but us.

"Yeah, yeah. Hey, the 2000s called and want your brain back," Jim answered, strolling over to sniff a snow-covered cement planter.

"You can't possibly need to pee again," I told it, taking the last of our luggage, Drake having carried in the other pieces a few minutes ago. "You watered five different planters already."

"Just checkin' it for good smells," Jim said, stomping its way over to the entrance.

"I know all about Whamageddon." Stella walked alongside me toward the entrance doors, all perky young Guardian filled with enthusiasm for her new apprenticeship. And lucky, lucky me, I was her mentor. "It's a game where you try to go from December first to the twenty-fourth without hearing the song 'Last Christmas' by Wham!"

"And István is cheating by trying to make me hear the song." Jim entered the airport, pausing to shake all the snow off its coat. "Bet he paid off that red dragon who drove us here."

"I'm sure István's not cheating. Do you have everything, Stella?" I asked, wheeling my bag as we entered after Jim and took a left toward the lounge set aside for those travelers who had their own private jets.

"Yes, I travel light, and I didn't want to check luggage on the flight over," Stella said, patting the duffel bag slung across her back. "And of course, I had my furniture sent to your London address."

I wanted badly to ask how much furniture she was bringing for the six months she would be shadowing me, Guardian-wise, but decided that was a subject to broach once we were back home. "I'm just sorry you had to go to the expense of flying all this way only to have to turn around immediately."

She shrugged. "It was only a few hours. I would have liked to see the other dragons, but it's still exciting to see Mr. Drake. And your children are green dragons, yes?"

"Yes," I said slowly, eyeing her as we approached the private lounge. Although I'd been acquainted with Stella for only an hour, I'd already determined she had a passionate interest in dragons that made me feel a bit itchy. "They're staying with my uncle right now. He's *not* a dragon."

"Oh," she said, sounding slightly disappointed, although she cheered up a few seconds later. "Still, dragon children will be interesting to see."

"You don't know the spawn," Jim said, shaking its shaggy black head. "Ash, István hid my noise-canceling headphones before he left. He wants me to hear the song. If you were a real demon lord, you'd banish him to the Akasha."

"I *am* a real demon lord, and I am *not* getting into this with you right now," I answered, giving another paranoid glance around us, but the main lounge was almost empty, probably twenty people in various states of airport ennui slumped in the plastic orange chairs. Added to the general sense of isolation and emptiness was the fact that half the small airport was off-limits, since it was under construction to add new runways and a new terminal. "I have enough on my plate keeping Drake from going ballistic."

Jim waited at the door to the private-jet customer lounge, silent until one of the lounge crew, zipping up a parka with one hand while clutching a pair of snowshoes with the other, hurried past us with a worried expression. "What else is new? Drake's always going drama llama over something lately."

"That's because there's a lot of crap going down right now, what with the trouble between the weyr and ouroboros tribes, not to mention having been away from the kids for three days. You know how he gets when we're away from them."

Jim nodded. "He thinks they're going to forget him. Like they could do that. He calls them all the time."

"He's just a devoted father," I said, sighing with relief when we entered the private lounge and I saw Drake stacking the luggage he'd hauled in a few minutes before. He was obviously about to return to help me when we entered, and instead gave me a nod before striding over to the reception desk that sat in front of floor-to-ceiling windows overlooking the jet hangars.

"Aisling," Jim said with a cock of its furry black eyebrow. "Dude made the nanny hold up the phone last night so he could watch the kids sleeping."

I made a little face, admitting, "Yeah, all right, that was a bit much, but there's nothing wrong with being a protective, caring parent concerned with our kids' welfare. Besides, no sane parent wants to be away from their kids so close to Christmas. He is a bit angsty about that, too."

"I've heard dragons are very intense in their emotions," Stella said, studying me as if I were a particularly interesting insect she had pinned to a board.

"*Creepy* is the word you're looking for," Jim said, then spun around, its nose in the air. "Oooh, I smell snackies!"

"Don't you dare eat anything until I make sure it's OK for us to do so," I warned it as it hustled forward, aware that there was only one attendant in the lounge, on the phone, while in front of him, Drake was clearly chewing him out. "Shit."

"*Merde,*" Jim automatically corrected. We watched as Drake gesticulated wildly. Although the dragon of my dreams possessed a passionate nature that literally left scorch marks on untreated furniture and structures, normally he kept his emotions in check when in public.

"I better go see what's got him riled up," I said, pointing to a spot in front of a deep leather armchair. "Sit there, and do not get on the chairs or couches. Yes, that's an order."

"Yes, Your Grinchy Majesty," Jim murmured, managing to make a sarcastic bow while plopping itself down next to the bags I'd dropped.

"I think I'll just type up my notes on my tablet," Stella said, sitting next to Jim.

I paused, glancing back at her. "You have notes already? We haven't talked about anything Guardian yet."

She gave me a toothy smile. "I like to document everything. It makes me feel like my brain is tidy if I take notes."

"Er … all right. Jim, stop trying to remove your bib. I don't want to have to pay the airport to clean up because you are extra drooly."

"Shouldn't have had that vet clean my teeth yesterday," it answered, sucking its teeth with an obnoxious noise. "They feel different."

"If you would let me brush your teeth like a reasonable demon, then I wouldn't have had to rush you to the vet to remove that dried piece of turkey jerky stuck in your molars."

"You're not a dentist," Jim said, making another tooth-sucking noise. "Like I trust you to poke around my teeth with toothpicks? Nuh-uh. And I told you that if you find a toothpaste that doesn't taste like mud, then I'll consider letting you brush my choppers."

"I don't have time for this argument now," I told it. "Just sit there and be good."

"Pfft. Like I can be anything but that?" It looked over at Stella, who was tapping industriously on her tablet. "Hey, did I ever tell you what I did to get kicked out of Abaddon?"

"Trouble in paradise?" I asked Drake a few seconds later. I glanced at my watch. "It's nothing to do with the children, is it? It's only been two hours since I checked in with Uncle Damian, and he said the kids were just heading to bed after having a *Star Wars* marathon."

"The children are fine," Drake answered, glaring at the man in front of us. The poor guy looked like he was about twenty, and wore the uniform of the concierge service that dealt with the high-end customers zooming in and out of this admittedly rural part of Canada—evidently the fishing here was deemed world-class—but was now visibly wilting under Drake's imposing presence. "What is *not* fine is the fact that Matteo was correct that our flight plan has not been approved. If we wait much longer, the storm will be upon us."

"I'm sorry, Mr. Vireo," the attendant said with a bob of his pronounced Adam's apple. "But your pilot was told that the Area Control Centre has grounded planes in our vicinity due to the storm. It's due to pass in a few hours, but until we get the all clear, the NAV is not approving flight plans originating from this airport. I believe your plane's crew has already been moved to the airport hotel."

Drake's bright green eyes narrowed on the man. "Then they can return, and the authorities must grant our flight plan. It is imperative that we leave immediately. We have children in our home in London awaiting our arrival."

"I'm sorry, sir, there's nothing we can do." The attendant gestured toward the window. Snow was falling fast and furious, which wouldn't have been worrisome in itself except it was starting to take on a horizontal aspect, a sign that a full-fledged blizzard was about to descend upon us. "No planes are allowed in or out of the Averas Airport at this time. If you like, I can try to book a room for your party at the airport hotel, although since the flight crews and almost all of the commercial passengers have been shuttled over there already, I can't guarantee anything."

"And there's nowhere else we could go?" I asked, putting a hand on Drake's arm, since I could feel his dragon fire rising at his obvious frustration with the situation.

"I'm afraid not," the attendant said, glancing worriedly at Drake. "Naturally, you are welcome to all the amenities here at the Averas FBO. We pride ourselves on our five-star service—although currently there is only me in the lounge, and I will be leaving in five minutes to go to the hotel—but I'm authorized to give you every comfort we can provide before I leave. We have a variety of free snacks and beverages on the far wall where your dog is, on-site security … although I think they've gone to the hotel, too … a climate-controlled hangar for your plane, and of course the best customer service in Ontario."

The young man tried to offer a confident smile, but it came out worried and unsure.

Drake wasn't having any of it. "That is not good enough. We need to leave now. You will inform the air traffic controllers that they are to make an exception for our plane. I will take responsibility for the safety of our travel."

"I don't know, sweetie," I said, squeezing his arm, more than a little worried about the weather. "If it's that dangerous out, maybe we shouldn't fly."

"The children are expecting us," he told me, his gorgeous face working with suppressed annoyance and anger. "It is almost Christmas Eve, and we told them we would be home then."

"I know, and I don't want to miss the fun any more than you do, but I'd rather get there in one piece. In the big picture of things, it won't matter if we're a few hours late."

Drake didn't like that, but I knew he wasn't about to do anything rash. "Very well," he said. "We will take three rooms at the hotel."

"Oh, I don't think—" The concierge bit back his protest at the look Drake shot him, and picked up the phone, murmuring, "I'll see if there're any rooms left."

"I have a bad feeling about this," I said to no one in particular as I wandered back to the couch where Stella was tucking away her tablet.

"About the snow?" She looked out the window. "It does look like it's getting windy. Could we get to the Ottawa portal shop?"

"The storm is coming from Ottawa, unfortunately. We looked into going to the portal shop rather than flying—despite the fact that dragons would rather cut off a limb than use a portal—but it had closed down because of the weather." I turned when the door opened behind me, and smiled at the sight of the two people who entered.

"I was hoping you guys got out," I said as May and Gabriel came in, covered in snow. "I thought you were leaving earlier?"

"We tried, but our flight plan was denied due to inclement weather," Gabriel said, glancing over at Drake, his eyebrows rising. "It would seem that you are suffering from the same situation."

"Unfortunately, yes."

"We went to find a hotel, but the car got stuck in the snow just as we got to the outer parking area, so we had to abandon it and trek in," May said, shaking the snow off her coat. "Gabriel wanted to bunk with our flight crew, but they are evidently crammed six to a room with your crew, and there's simply no free space for even one more person."

"Damn." I bit my lower lip in thought. "Joining Matteo and the rest of our crew was going to be my next suggestion."

"I'm afraid that's a lost cause," May said, glancing at Stella when the latter moved over next to me, her eyes alight with interest.

"And there's only the one hotel?" I asked.

"Apparently," May answered. "We thought there might be another one, but couldn't find anything but snow. Hello."

"Sorry, I should have introduced you. May Northcott, this is Stella Pendleton. She's going to apprentice with me for the next six months." I gave the latter a big smile that I hoped looked sincere. "We ran across her on the way to the airport."

"Not literally, of course. I was coming to see the gathering of dragons which Miss Aisling said was happening. I was very sorry to miss it," Stella said, holding out her hand when I introduced Gabriel to her.

"Gabriel is the silver wyvern," I added. "They live in Australia, which must seem like heaven right about now, what with this weather."

"It most certainly does," May agreed, her eyes amused when Gabriel, who had finished stacking their luggage next to ours, moved over to Drake, obviously to discuss the hotel situation. "I wonder if the others got out safely before the snow hit?"

"I have no clue. I assume so, or we'd have seen them here," I said, watching Drake. He greeted Gabriel pleasantly enough, but he still looked irate.

"Your husband is very handsome," Stella told May, whose eyes widened in response. "I had no idea dragons could have dimples. And his accent is quite pleasant. Was he born in Australia?"

"Yes. His dad is African, and his mom is from Australia," May answered, giving me a look that was brimming with amusement. "And his dimples *are* delightful. I've thought so from the first day I met him."

"I've always had a soft spot for Gabriel since he's done so much for the green dragons," I said, hoping Stella would get the point.

"Like the time he poisoned you?" Jim asked, nosing a magazine out of the bag I'd set down, and managing to flick it open. "Yeah, that was super helpful."

"That incident aside, Gabriel has been a good friend to our sept." Feeling like it was worthwhile to warn Stella against acting on the fascination she obviously felt, I inquired with as much solemnity as I could, "I'm always amazed to see you get through security with the two daggers that you always seem to have hidden about your person, May. It must give you a lot of comfort knowing you can keep them close to hand in case they're needed."

"I shadow walk if I have to," May answered, her voice tight, no doubt with the effort to keep from laughing. "And yes, it does give me much comfort to have the daggers on me at all times."

I thought Stella's eyes were going to bug out of her head. Her fingers twitched. "You can shadow walk?"

May was about to answer when the door opened again, and a man stomped in while bitching in strident tones.

"If anyone told me that I would be trapped in this backwater hell pit unable to reach my mate just so I could discuss the latest threat from the tribes, I would have stayed home like that bastard Constantine," Kostya said, stopping in the middle of the room to strike a dramatic pose. Kostya was forever striking dramatic poses. May, Ysolde, and I all had a secret drinking game where we got a shot of whatever booze was handy whenever Kostya either posed or emoted dramatically. "Drake! Did you tell the airport that we must be allowed to fly out?"

Drake shot his brother a long-suffering look that had a whole lot less patience than normal. "I'm dealing with it, Kostya."

"Tell them that Aoife is waiting for me. She is tired of being at Bee's side without me to temper the madness coming from Constantine," Kostya added.

Drake spun around and spat something out in Zilant, the language used by dragons before English took over. Judging by the shocked look on Kostya's face, I assumed it was fairly rude. Kostya snarled something back that Drake ignored.

I slid a look at my watch and murmured to May, "Four o'clock. Surely that's not too early for a drink?"

She giggled in response.

"Who—" Stella started to say.

"That's Kostya, Drake's older brother. Kostya is wyvern of the black sept, and yes, he is normally that annoying. His mate, Aoife, is with her sister, Bee, who is mate to another wyvern. Bee is due to give birth any day, so Aoife decided to stay with her instead of coming out here with Kostya."

Stella pulled out her tablet, her voice hushed as she said softly, "So many dragons. And all of them are so handsome. I really must make more notes."

"You might write down that all of them are mated," May said, examining the tip of a dagger that suddenly appeared in her hand. "Happily so."

Stella eyed first the dagger, then Gabriel before turning her attention to the tablet.

"Have you tried to get a hotel room?" I asked Kostya.

"Yes. There are none. And the people who selfishly refused to yield one to me had me run out of the hotel for harassment," Kostya said, a little wisp of smoke curling out of his nose. "Me! It was ridiculous. I threatened no one with actual death. Just a little … unpleasantness."

"Yes, I'm sure that went over well," I said, biting back the urge to both laugh and yell at Kostya for being so pigheaded.

"I offered money. They still refused," he snapped, storming over to the window to glare out at the snow.

"Maybe we should try to get back to Rowan and Sophea's house if we can't fly out or get a hotel room," May said, looking worried.

"I don't know that we can. Our driver said his car was pretty good in the snow, but he was anxious to drop us off and hit the main roads before the streets became impassable," I told her.

May made a face. "I kind of hoped it was our rental car that left us stranded, but I see what you mean. It's snowing even harder now."

Stella made a little noise of question next to me. "Rowan is the red dragon wyvern, brother to Bee and Aoife. He was hosting the *sárkány* that we were all attending," I told Stella. "It was an emergency session due to some issues the dragonkin are having with other dragons, and since it was Rowan's first time being the official host, we all flew out to spend a couple of days here while they dealt with the situation."

"I really wish I could have seen the meetings," she said in a heavy sigh.

"There was a lot of bitching about ouroboros tribes," Jim said, looking up from its magazine. "And why some dude named Xavier is trying to off the dragonkin."

"It's too long to explain now," I told Stella when she looked to me for more explanation. "I'll tell you about it later. Suffice it to say that it's a pretty grave situation to drag everyone out right before Christmas."

Kostya had evidently reached the limit of nursing his grievances, because he spun around, his hands on his hips as he demanded, "Drake! Why are you not forcing the airport to let us fly out?"

"I did everything I could," Drake snapped, causing May and me to look at him in surprise. He and Gabriel joined our little group. "If you wish to try to change the laws, then by all means do so, but stop acting like a petulant child who expects me to do his work for him. Aisling, are you damp from taking Jim for a walk?"

"No, I'm fine. We were only outside a few minutes. But you're going to cause trouble if you don't tamp down your fire a bit," I said in a tone pitched for his ears only. I slid an arm around his waist, reveling in the feel of him next to me, happy despite the situation. "That poor kid who was left to cope on his own is going to have a hissy fit if you set fire to the fancy passengers' area."

Kostya turned his bad temper on Gabriel. "I don't suppose you've done anything to help?"

"Other than picking your sorry ass out of the snow and driving you to the airport rather than letting you walk a mile when you crashed into a fence, no," Gabriel answered with a dangerous edge to his voice.

I pursed my lips at the comment, while May raised her eyebrows. If Drake was normally calm in public, Gabriel was always cheerful and pleasant.

"You crashed?" I asked, wondering if he had accident insurance on the expensive car he'd rented for the drive out to Rowan's house.

"Yes. I slid on black ice. And my ass is anything but sorry." Kostya said the last to Gabriel. "In fact, my mate tells me it is a magnificent thing, a pleasure to behold."

"The urge to praise Gabriel's ass is strong, and yet, I think I'm going to stay out of this," May murmured when Gabriel strode off to the restrooms.

"Good plan. Everyone's a bit on edge," I said with a glance at Drake. "May suggested that we might try to go back to Rowan's house. What do you think?"

"It's not possible." A muscle in his jaw twitched, never a good sign. "The snow will get worse before it gets better, and I doubt if we could get a car at this point. We will have to remain here."

"And you're sure the hotel is out?" I tried to keep my voice whine-free, but I admit the thought of being trapped at the airport with Kostya was making me a bit cranky. I wanted to be home with my children, so I could drink cocoa, sing Christmas carols, and watch Drake try very hard *not* to give in to the kids' entreaties to open presents early.

"Yes. Like Kostya, I offered a financial enticement—minus the threats—but they refuse to accommodate us."

"They told us they were making people room together, because they had so many stranded travelers," Gabriel said as he returned to our group. "I think we're going to have to make the best of the situation here."

"I agree." I kept my gaze on Drake. "I just hope the storm is over quickly, because my uncle said he's considering giving the twins whiskey and cigars to calm them down if we don't get back soon."

"Both sound delightful right now. So does beating up Kostya." Gabriel cracked his knuckles.

"I understand exactly how you feel," I murmured.

Fire blossomed at the tips of my feet. I tamped it out with the toe of my boot while Jim snickered to itself.

"I just said I *understood* the urge," I told Drake. "You can't tell me you don't want to punch him out right now, too."

He opened his mouth to answer, but Kostya stopped next to him, moodily asking, "Who are you going to punch? Constantine? Baltic? I'm up for either. Or both. Preferably both."

"That's all we need—you storming around bitching about them. We've put up with it for three days. Why don't you give it a rest?" Gabriel asked, his voice once again sharp and unlike his normal smooth tone. "We're all tired of you and your insistence on clinging to the past."

Instantly, Kostya bristled up. "I will not stand for this treatment! I am a wyvern, not some minor dragonling you can so insult," Kostya snarled before turning to Drake. "I suppose you are in agreement? I should have known the day would come when you would turn on the black dragons. Your own kin!"

"Yes, because I've tried to destroy them my entire fucking life!" Drake almost yelled at his brother.

"Two drinks, I think," May whispered to me.

"Whoa," Jim said, its eyes round. I knew just how it felt. Drake didn't often swear in public, and seldom at his brother in front of other dragons. "Someone's buttons are on a hair trigger today."

"Be silent unless you are invited to speak," Drake told Jim.

"You're not the boss of me, Aisling is," Jim started to say, then yelped when its tail burst into flames, and immediately scooted on its butt to put it out.

Drake said something rude in Magyar, and marched across the room to where the bathrooms were clearly marked.

"I hope he splashes himself with a little water to cool off," I said under my breath.

Kostya seemed as shocked as the rest of us by Drake's short temper.

"I never accused him of harming the black dragons—" Kostya told Gabriel, then obviously realized he was seeking sympathy from his once-hated (now barely tolerated) enemy, and scowled at the room in general before stalking over to the window to stare out at the driving snow again.

Gabriel's jaw flexed; then he murmured something about calling Maata and Tipene, his guards, who were at home ensuring the safety of the silver dragons, and moved off to a corner.

"Yikes," May said.

"You said it."

"This is all so fascinating," Stella said, her eyes following Drake. "I had no idea that dragons were so … raw."

I managed to keep from saying anything rude, instead giving a little shiver. "Ugh. I'm starting to get cold. Think I'll dig out a sweater."

I knelt at our mound of suitcases while May did the same; then she went to visit the ladies' room.

When I was clad in a warm sweater, I noticed the young man at the concierge desk had evidently made his escape out another door as the coat, scarf, and hat that had been laid across one end of the reception counter were missing, along with him. Since the hotel was at the edge of the airport property, I figured he probably trekked out across the parking lot on foot.

Five minutes later, Drake returned with his temper once again in hand. I'd set Jim's waterproof jacket over by a heating vent so it could dry, and hung up Drake's coat on a stand behind the concierge desk. Mine was draped over a chair, since it was wetter than his after I'd walked Jim around so it could potty.

"It looks like we're going to be together a bit longer," I said once I was done arranging things to dry, assessing the lounge. "I wonder if there are any blankets and pillows to be had?"

A muscle in Drake's jaw flexed a couple of times, but at last he had to give in to the inevitable. "I will go look for blankets. Kostya! Stop glaring at the snow and help me search the airport."

"Protective, too," I heard Stella whisper to herself. "That's attractive in a male."

"Now I am to be ordered to do menial tasks?" Kostya grumbled, spinning around. "I am a wyvern, not a servant!"

"We're all dragons, Aisling's student aside, and I doubt if even she would see the mates suffer from cold because she was above finding resources for their comfort," Drake told him.

"Oh." Stella tucked away her tablet and straightened up. "I'd be happy to go with you, Mr. Drake."

"There's no need; I wouldn't want it said that I didn't do my part," Kostya almost snarled as he stalked past her, following Drake out of the lounge.

"Are there any unmarried dragons?" Stella asked, her gaze once again on Gabriel.

"Loads, but all the wyverns are taken," May answered, looking like she wanted to pull out a dagger again.

"But now there are the tribe masters to take into consideration," I said, thinking of the trouble that was casting a black cloud over the weyr.

"That's right," May said, looking a lot less dagger-ish. "Only one of them is mated that we know of."

"Two, counting Bastian," I pointed out.

"Yes." We were both silent for a minute, thinking with sadness of the loss of the blue dragons from the weyr.

"These tribes … they're like your septs?" Stella asked us in a hushed tone.

"Kind of. They're groups of dragons who band together in a tribe. They aren't necessarily the same type of dragon—blue, red, black, etc. And their leaders are called masters instead of wyverns," May explained.

"We've met a couple of masters. One is extremely annoying," I said slowly, my mind still troubled by what would happen between the tribes and the weyr. The wyverns themselves couldn't come to any decision at the *sárkány* other than to hold firm to the temporary laws they'd put into place at the re-forming of the weyr a few months before.

"Are they as … imposing … as the wyverns?" Stella asked.

"Oh yes." May smiled at me.

I returned the gesture. "Once a dragon leader, always a dragon leader. Well. I suppose we should look around the lounge and see what we have to work with."

"I hope we can keep Kostya and Gabriel apart," May said as she shed her coat, hanging it with Gabriel's on the coatrack. "Gabriel's temper seems to be as short as Drake's."

"At least we only have to deal with the three of them," I said, trying to rally my somewhat depressed spirits. "It would be a hundred times worse if—"

"By the rood, it's insanity out there!" The door opened again to reveal a willowy blond woman, followed immediately by a tall, lanky young man. "Are you all stuck, too? They said we couldn't fly out. Brom, see if you can get reception here. Baltic is going to go stark, staring mad if we can't reach Pavel soon."

"Ysolde, mate of Baltic, wyvern of the light dragons, and her son, Brom," I said quietly to Stella, who had scooted over next to me, her face awash with pleasure and amazement. "Just an FYI: Baltic is the son of the First Dragon, the demigod who created the race of dragons, so do not do anything to piss off him or Ysolde."

Stella's eyebrows arched, and for a moment, I thought she was going to say something, but instead, she dipped her head and tapped on her tablet.

Ysolde marched over to where we were standing, pulling off a red beret and shaking the snow off her thick red wool, ankle-length coat. "I don't suppose there's hot tea to be had?"

"I'm sure there is over at the—Jim!" I rushed past where Baltic was dragging two wheeled suitcases.

"The snow is thigh-deep, and coming down even harder," Ysolde called as she moved over to peer into Brom's cell phone.

Baltic stood and surveyed the room for a few seconds before heaving an audible sigh, and deposited the suitcases next to a small cluster of chairs that sat around a round table, the antagonistic look he shot the back of Gabriel's head implying he was staking out his territory.

I pulled Jim away from the array of pastries, muffins, cookies, and popcorn that were laid out on a hospitality table.

"Please tell me you didn't eat all that," I said, pointing at the muffin and cookie wrappers in the trash basket. "Because I'm tired of trying to come up with excuses for the vet about why you aren't losing weight on your diet food."

"A demon has to live," Jim said with a sniffle. "This magnificent form isn't going to maintain itself on that crap food you let the vet talk you into. I need calories! Proteins! Carbs galore, along with various succulent meats, and let us not forget all those sweet, sweet fats that keep my coat in such glorious form!"

I narrowed my eyes on my demon in dog form, and mopped up its slobbery chops with one of the many drool cloths I carried. "If you ate any chocolate, you're going to find yourself out in the snow barfing it all up, and don't think I didn't bring that medicine that makes you puke, because I did."

Jim backed away from me, trying hard to look martyred. "Man, you make one little slipup with a chocolate Easter bunny, and all Abaddon breaks loose."

"One," I said, ticking off my finger as May approached, "you might be a demon, but chocolate is still poisonous to your doggy form. Two, you took candy from an actual child. And three, that child was my daughter, so yes, all Abaddon will break loose if you eat stuff you aren't supposed to. How many muffins did you eat, and which cookies?"

Jim rolled its eyes, and strolled over to May, rubbing its furry black Newfoundland head on her leg. "Just two banana nut muffins, and none of the cookies. And a couple of bags of popcorn."

I looked at the red-and-white striped paper bags filled with popcorn, then down at the trash. "I don't see any of the bags."

Jim whistled through its teeth and looked off into the distance.

"Right, new rule. No eating paper bags. You don't know where they were made, and it can't be good for you to eat paper. I don't see any alcohol here, May, so we may have to dip into the bottle of dragon's blood wine that Drake has stashed in his luggage."

"Did someone say dragon's blood?" Ysolde asked, coming over to eye the goodies. "Oooh, snickerdoodles. Baltic loves those. I'll set one aside for him, if you don't mind."

"You might as well. I think we're going to be here for a while."

We all turned when the door opened, and Drake and Kostya returned empty-handed.

"No luck finding any blankets or pillows?" I asked.

Drake looked pissed again, much to my dismay. "None. There are a handful of mortals bunking down in the inhabitable part of the terminal, but I couldn't bring myself to take the few blankets they had. This lounge is much warmer, and we have extra clothing we can wear if needed."

"And snacks," I pointed out. "Can I get you something? The selection isn't great, but it should keep starvation at bay."

He shook his head and, after pausing to speak for a minute to Gabriel, moved off to the other side of the room, pulling out his cell phone again.

Kostya headed for a chair next to the window, pausing long enough to look daggers at Baltic, who ignored him.

I returned to where May and Ysolde were softly chatting, Stella making more notes at a chair next to the heating vent.

"I take it the pickings were slim?" May asked when I reached them.

"Zero, in fact. Sounds like we're doing significantly better here than out in the main part of the terminal, so I guess we should count ourselves lucky."

"At least the muffins are fresh," Ysolde said around a mouthful of orange-cranberry muffin. "And Brom said the weather station is predicting the storm should move off by morning. We'll barely make it home in time to spend Christmas Eve with family, but it should be doable assuming the weather acts like it's supposed to."

"How are Pavel and Holland doing?" I asked.

Ysolde sighed, and slid a glance toward Baltic, who was tapping on his phone, no doubt trying to send texts. "They're nervous wrecks. Amaranthe was due yesterday, and although the doctor said she's fine, they're both convinced that something will happen to their baby."

It took me a few seconds to sort out the confusion of pronouns in Ysolde's sentence, but at last I worked it out. "I'd be worried, too, if my sister was having a baby for me and my partner. Be sure to let us know when the baby is born, so the green dragons can send a present to the newest light dragon."

Ysolde sighed a second time, a flash of ire in her eyes that took me by surprise. "Yes, well, currently that title is being held by Brom."

I felt a presence at my side, and gave in to Stella's pleading look to whisper to her, "I told you that Brom was Ysolde's son. Baltic is his dad in every sense but biologically."

Ysolde had very good hearing, a fact I forget now and again.

"Yes, and his stepgrandfather is a big old pushy pain in the ass." She eyed Stella while I hurriedly introduced her.

"Ysolde is the only one who refers to the First Dragon that way," May said with a chirrup of laughter.

"Well, he *is* a pain," Ysolde insisted, telling Stella, "The First Dragon has been pestering Brom for years to make him a light dragon, but I thought we were past the worst of it. Then one morning about three weeks ago, I woke up to find Brom breathing fire all over the kitchen, and informing me he'd decided that he wanted to be a dragon after all, and who should visit him the second—*the very second*—he decided that, but the First Pain in the Ass." She took a deep breath. "So now Brom is learning how to dragon, and Baltic is both pleased that he made this decision and annoyed that his father interfered despite knowing I wasn't keen on the idea. But what are you going to do? In the end, what matters is that Brom is happy."

We all looked at Brom, who was slumped in a chair the way only teens could manage. He was reading something on his phone and looked anything but happy, but I chalked that up to teenage malaise and not an unhappiness at his decision.

"That is what's important. Is he going to go to college?" I asked.

"Yes, in England, which is why we're living at Dragonwood for a while."

"We're going to be in London for a bit, too. Drake wants to go back to Hungary, but I have to stay in England for six months for Guardians' Guild business. Pal is ecstatic, since it means he and Nora can spend so much time together—that's where he is, May. I meant to tell you when you asked about him yesterday, but then everyone started shouting about that bastard Deus, and I forgot. Regardless, we'll be able to visit each other frequently, Ysolde."

"We're going to stay in London for the next month or so, as well," May said. "We'll have to start up the Mates Union lunches again."

"Oooh, yes, that would be nice. We've been so spread apart the last few years. And of course, now there are more mates to join us," Ysolde said, her eyes narrowing in thought. "I'm happy to host the first meeting. Salmon en croûte, I think. With fresh lemon asparagus, and some of those delicious cheddar sage biscuits that Pavel makes …"

"Ysolde does the best hosting," May told Stella. "I always come away at least five pounds heavier, but oh, so happy."

"Hands down, she's the best," I agreed, glancing across the room to where I assumed Drake and Gabriel would be chatting, but to my surprise, all the dragons were spread out. Gabriel was reading a book; Drake stood at one window, while Kostya resumed his stance (dramatic) at another one. Baltic had moved over to examine Brom's phone. I gathered neither was getting good reception.

"That's not good," I said softly.

The others looked. "Definitely not," Ysolde said.

"Gabriel's been nervy, and that's not at all like him," May commented.

"Is something amiss?" Stella asked.

"The men are twitchy," Ysolde said, absently eating popcorn. "You know what that means."

I made a face.

May smiled.

Stella looked confused, then resigned. "I do?"

"After the arguments at the *sárkány*, it's needed," I pointed out.

"When do we let them do it?" May asked.

"Do what?" Stella asked, her brows pulling together. "What am I supposed to know but don't?"

"The storm is due to hit shortly. If they wear themselves out too early, they'll just tense back up. I say we have them hold on as long as we can bear it," Ysolde said with a calmness that I knew came from centuries of dealing with fractious dragons.

Stella clicked her tongue, tugging at my arm. "What—"

"The wyverns tend to get a bit uptight. It's part of their nature, you understand," Ysolde explained. "They feel things so much more than others. And when they get stressed like that, we've found it's best to let them relieve the tension by beating the ever-living tar out of each other."

"Fists only," I told a shocked-looking Stella. "No claws, fire, or dragon form. Just mano a mano. They really seem to like it, oddly enough."

"But ... they're dragons," she protested. "They are immensely powerful. Surely you must worry that they will kill each other?"

"Oh, they know better than to go that far," Ysolde said, stirring a mug of hot tea. "They may knock out the odd tooth or two—"

"And someone always breaks Kostya's collarbone," I said, taking a pastry after making sure Jim was engaged in talking with Brom and Baltic.

"Yes, sometimes a rib or collarbone is broken, but they mend quickly," Ysolde agreed.

"And Gabriel is an awesome healer, so he takes care of any hurts that don't want to heal up fast," May said, eyeing the selection of fruit, putting an orange and some grapes on a plate, along with two muffins.

"It's all so … brutal," Stella said, shaking her head.

"Not really. They like it, and it clears the air, so we let them have ten minutes or so to work out the worst of their issues, and then everyone is reasonable again." I glanced around the room. "All in all, you have to admit that our situation isn't as horrible as it could be. Yes, we're stuck here, but our children are all safe and sound back home, and this isn't a bad little lounge. The chairs look comfy, and there's food, and they even have a Christmas tree and fake presents." We all looked at the corner next to the concierge desk where a tall tree twinkled merrily. "It's not where we want to be, but at least we have the whole place to ourselves, without strangers intruding and making things awkward."

Air swirled once again as the door opened, and three snow-covered people entered the room.

They were *not* dragons.

HOUR TWO
ALLIE

Stop it.

Stop being concerned about my Beloved? Christian gave what I can only describe as a mental snort. *I will be dead ten years before I stop worrying about you.*

And I appreciate that fact, but you can also stop treating me like I can't walk.

Your limp is worse than normal. "I believe that is the lounge, Finch. Perhaps you would see if the airline was correct in saying we can stay there."

I whomped Christian on his chest, which wasn't easy to do considering he had one arm around me, more or less hauling me through the airport, and also because I held the bags with presents for the kids, and six snow globes weighed a lot. "I told you to stop it. Don't listen to Christian, Finch, I'm perfectly fine and the lounge is only twenty yards away. The cold is bothering my leg a smidgen, but my limp is ever-present, as Mr. Fangs here knows."

Christian didn't even flinch at the "Mr. Fangs," which told me he was more concerned than he let on. And since my leg was hurting more than normal—it always did in extreme cold—I leaned into him and let him coddle me.

Finch hesitated, watching me with an abstracted expression before he moved into place on my other side and, despite being laden with both his luggage and our bags, held out a hand. "I'll take your bags."

"It's just snow globes for Josef and the twins," I told him, but handed over the bags. "And the ghosts, because they'd be hurt if I left them out. When did the airline people say our plane would be ready to go?"

"It's ready, but evidently flights are not being allowed out due to the snow," Christian answered.

"Not even the expensive zippy jet that you hired?" I gave a little shrug. "I would have thought that thing could fly in any weather, but I suppose it's better to be safe than sorry."

"If there was any way we could get out of here safely, I would take it, but disappointing as it is to miss the girls' Christmas play, we will have to make do," Christian said. I heard a whisper of a comment in his mind that had me giggling to myself.

Just admit you don't want to see the play, I told him.

What makes you think that?

One, our girls have zero ability to sing, despite stomping around the house singing Christmas songs at full volume for the last four weeks.

They just need some training, he said, but the thought faltered as soon as he started it.

I did laugh then, pausing to kiss the corner of his mouth, which was all I could reach given how many layers of clothing we all wore. "Thank you for not blaming my side of the family for the twins' lack of musical ability. I am fully aware that you and Finch sing like birds. Oh, no pun intended, Finch."

"None taken," he said, as serene as ever.

"Naturally, I would have enjoyed seeing the Christmas play, if for no other reason than Sebastian's boys are sure to wreak havoc on it." Christian's voice was rich with amusement despite our situation.

"Yes, well, I can't argue with that," I said, wishing I could curl up with a heating pad. "They are hellions. I just hope Josef doesn't pick up any bad habits from them. Do you think there's food in the lounge? My stomach is saying rude things to me about missing lunch."

Christian heaved one of his martyred sighs. He was a master at them. "I told you that we could take the time for you to eat."

"You did, but I thought it was more important to try to beat the storm to the airport, and look where that's gotten us. Oh, good, there it is. Fingers crossed there's something to nom on."

Christian opened the door for me, and I took five steps in before stopping, more than a little surprised that the room was fully occupied. *Dammit. There's a bunch of people here. Crap.*

Those aren't people, Christian said slowly, his mind full of wariness that I'd never felt in him.

"Uh … hello," I said when everyone stopped and turned to stare at us. *They look like people.*

But they aren't, Christian said, then strode forward, and said in what I thought of as his extra-bossy voice, "I am C. J. Dante, head of the Moravian Council. My Beloved needs warmth and a place to rest. We want no trouble, but I insist that she be allowed to remain here."

Wow, really? You went straight to antagonistic?

Stay behind me, Allegra. You do not know who they are.

Yeah, and we're not likely to with you being all bristly.

"What my husband means to say—but forgot because we've been out in the cold for what seems like days—is, hi, I'm Allie and he's Christian, and this is Finch, and if you don't mind, we'd like to hang out here until the blizzard passes," I said, moving over to where Christian stood as stiff as a board. "Our plane was grounded, which I assume is the case with you all, as well."

"Moravian Council?" A tall man with a sweep of dark hair, and the brightest green eyes I'd ever seen, moved over to stand next to a woman with shoulder-length curly brown hair. "You are Dark Ones?"

"We are," Christian said just as stiffly as his posture, and I had a suspicion he was a minute away from demanding I leave the room.

A minute is far too long. Would you leave if I asked you?

No. What's wrong with you? I asked. *Why are you acting so formal?*

"I am Drake Vireo," the tall man said, making one of the bows that Christian did so well. To my surprise, he did it with almost as much panache. "This is my mate, Aisling Grey. Naturally, we will not deny your mate warmth if she is injured."

"I am a healer, if I can be of service," another man said. This one had warm brown skin, a wild tangle of hair that reached past his shoulders, and a close-cropped goatee. But it was his eyes that made me do a double take. They were a brilliant silver, just like Christian's. He, also, made a bow, and added, "I am Gabriel Tauhou, wyvern of the silver sept. This is my mate, May Northcott."

"Whoa, vampires?"

I stared in complete disbelief when a large black Newfoundland dog shambled forward, gave Finch's shoes a sniff, then turned his attention to us.

Did that dog just talk, or did the cold freeze my brain?
It is not a dog.

"Been a long time since I've seen any of you guys. Hiya, Jim's the name. Effrijim, really, but that's just not my style, you know?" the dog said, giving my knees a friendly snuffle before plopping down in front of me. "You don't smell like a girl vamp. What are you? Vespillo? Necromancer?"

"Summoner," I answered, wondering if I'd lost my mind.

"Knew it was something ghosty. I'm a demon sixth class, in case you were wondering, and I think the ways your eyes are bugging out means you are. Cool eyes, by the way. I like the way they don't match."

"Thank you," I said, not knowing what else to say. *A demon? Are we in danger?*

Not from it. It appears to be bound to the woman who is approaching.

"Jeezumcrow, Jim, you don't just go up and startle people like that. I've told you before that not everyone is copacetic with you being in dog form. Hi, Allie, was it? I'm Aisling, as Drake mentioned. He's the wyvern of the green dragons, as you probably guessed. Shall I do the rest of the introductions?" She rattled off a bunch of names as she indicated the others in the room.

Dragons? Now I know the snow did a number on me. She did say dragons, didn't she?

Yes. These are dragons. He was silent for a moment. *All of them. They must have had some gathering. Normally you don't find more than a few of them gathered together, and the demon's handler just named four of them.*

Wow. "I'm sorry to look so stunned, Jim, but I've never seen a demon in dog form before. Or dragons in person."

"Don't worry, we don't bite," another woman said, an elegant blond woman who flashed a friendly smile. "Well, we do, but only in the privacy of our own homes. Come sit over here by the heating vent, Allie. I'm Ysolde, in case you didn't catch the name. You look half-frozen. Do you like tea? They have a nice selection of herbal varieties, if so, and Brom—that's my son, the one over there poured into the chair like he has no bones in his body—just refilled the electric kettle, so the water is hot."

Beloved, I insist that you stay by my side where I can protect you.

"Thanks, I'd love a cup of tea," I said, following Ysolde as she led me over to a comfy chair. "I've never seen dragons before. Are you guys having a party, or something? And what's a sept?"

Allegra! I just told you not to leave my side! Christian stormed after me, scattering looks that were unfriendly at best.

Yeah, and you know how much I love it when you give me orders. Calm down, Christian. These people aren't going to hurt us.

You don't know that. They're dragons! Dragons are notoriously volatile.

The guys might be—I'll admit they look a bit intense—but they have their wives with them, and you know full well that we make even the most annoying of beings behave.

He sighed into my head, and I could feel him thinking several rude things, but we'd been together long enough for him to keep most of them just out of my mental reach.

Most of them.

"Not a party, but a gathering," Ysolde answered. "And a sept is more or less a collective noun for specific dragons. For instance, Baltic and I are in the light dragon sept."

"That's so interesting," I said, shifting until my leg was propped up on a small ottoman. "I had no idea you guys separated yourselves that way. We just have vamps."

"And yet you are here in the backside of Ontario," the grumpy dragon named Kostya said, shooting a suspicious look at Christian. "I can't help but wonder why."

"Not that it is any of your business, our jet developed engine troubles, and we were directed to this airport to hire one, since there were none available in Ottawa." Christian's beautiful eyes were almost as antagonistic as his attitude.

It was a valid question, I pointed out. *You, yourself, groused about having to come to a backwater airport just to hire a jet while ours is getting fixed.*

I did not grouse. I complained. And I was unaware that this minuscule airport was evidently the destination of rich mortals who hunt and fish, and thus has a company providing private jets for hire, he answered.

"Are you injured?" the silver-eyed Gabriel asked, moving toward me, but stopping when Christian spun around and glared at him.

"No, I have a wonky leg, but other than it being a bit stiff due to the cold, I'm fine."

"Your leg is not wonky," Christian said quickly. "It is simply shorter than the other one."

I've never seen you like this. Why are you acting this way?

They're dragons.

So? They don't have a vendetta against vamps, do they?

Not that I know of, but I wouldn't put it past them. They are primal beings, not urbane and sophisticated as we are.

I took a look around the room. *I don't know—they all seem pretty urbane to me. They certainly are demonstrating better manners than you are at this moment.*

Ysolde brought me a cup of tea, while Aisling bustled over with a plate of fruit and pastries, followed by her demon dog. "So," she said brightly after handing me the plate, sidling past where Christian had taken up a protective stance, Finch flanking him. "I've never met a vampire before. I've heard about you guys, of course. I'm a Guardian, by the way. That's how I ended up with Jim."

"Oh, we know a Guardian," I said, giving Christian a fast scowl until he, with an annoyed *tsk*, stopped hovering and dragged one of the armchairs over next to mine. Finch, clearly not as worried about the dragons as his uncle, sat down at a table and pulled out his laptop. "Her name is Noelle. We met her a long time ago, but she was very helpful when we had a problem with some demons invading Christian's house. Do you know her?"

"Noelle," Aisling said slowly, her lips pursed in thought. "I'm afraid the name isn't familiar, but I don't know a lot of the Guardians. I was mostly self-trained, and when I did find a mentor, she kind of had to come to me because—" She waved her hand toward where the male dragons were now clustered, periodically shooting glimpses toward Christian and Finch. "Being a wyvern's mate takes up a lot of time, so I don't get to mingle with other Guardians much."

"I know how that goes," I said, sipping the tea, reveling in the sensation of my body slowly thawing with the heat of the beverage. "Christian is the head of the vampire collective, as he said, and that means he's forever going hither and yon taking care of business. I used to stay home because of the kids—my twins are very inventive when it comes to doing things they shouldn't do—but now that they're older, I'm able to travel with him. We were just in BC visiting Finch's friend and his Beloved."

"You have twins?" Aisling smiled broadly. "So do I! A boy and a girl. They're nine, and a handful, let me tell you. Our youngest is three."

"Mine are eight, and both girls," I said, feeling a kinship with this woman despite the circumstances. "Our oldest boy just turned twelve."

Ysolde, who had been consulting with the one man who hadn't clustered up with the other dragons, returned and gave Christian such a pointed look that, to my complete surprise, he rose from the chair and offered it to her.

A woman with black hair cut in a flapper bob followed her, sitting on her heels next to the demon dog. "Are we talking kids?" Ysolde asked. "Baltic and I have two. Our son is home with Baltic's lieutenant and his mate, who are expecting their first child any minute now."

"I remember my first," I said with a little laugh, relieved when Christian, evidently deciding I was safe talking with the women, joined Finch at his table. "I had no idea how much it was going to change my life. Do you have children, er … ? Sorry, there were so many names."

"May," the flapper woman said, then smiled. "No. We're not in any hurry, despite Gabriel's mother making some pretty broad hints as to how happy she would be to act as a midwife for me. His sister has three daughters, and we enjoy having them visit a few times a year, so that satisfies our maternal and paternal needs for now."

"Smart thinking," Ysolde said, nodding. "Well, now that the family stuff is done, can we talk about the elephant in the room?"

The short woman with a shoulder-length bob, whom Aisling had introduced as her apprentice Stella, looked around, a bit startled. "There's an elephant here, too?"

"I was speaking metaphorically," Ysolde said, tucking her legs beneath her on the chair. "I meant vampires. We want to know all about you. Are we going to have to fend you off if you suddenly get hungry? Are the movies true and you have no reflection?"

"Does the sun fry you to a crisp?" Aisling asked.

"Can you guys fly? I've always wanted to fly," May said.

"I thought dragons had wings?" I asked, momentarily sidetracked.

"Pfft," she said, waving away the idea. "That's just weird medieval thinking. Dragon form has no wings."

"It does a have a tail, though," Ysolde said, then suddenly frowned. "And some have tiny, stupidly small T. rex arms."

"I'm sure your dragon arms were just fine," Aisling said, reaching across me to pat Ysolde, adding, "She's a bit touchy on the subject of her dragon-form arms."

"So would you be if the First Dragon made sure your arms were ineffective," she said with a sniff, and a glare at her husband, who did a double take before frowning back at her.

"To answer your questions, no, we're not likely to attack in a bloodlust," I said with a little laugh. "For one, I don't drink blood. Finch does, but I gather he topped up this morning before we set off. Christian can only feed from me, so all is well there. The sun isn't nice to Finch, but Christian and I are Joined, which means we have a bond, so he can tolerate it a lot more than other, unmated vampires. And they have reflections; they can go into churches, and don't mind garlic, not that you asked about those, but I assume they were coming."

"This is fascinating," Ysolde said, absently taking a pastry from my plate. "I had no idea that you guys were so similar to the dragonkin."

"Oh?" I asked.

She said around a mouthful of raspberry croissant, "The mate thing—that's a life bond with dragons. I assume it is with vampires, too?"

"Oh, definitely," I answered.

"How did you guys get started?" Aisling asked. "The dragon race was formed by a god—"

"Demigod pain in the—never mind," Ysolde said, sliding me a look that made me want to laugh.

"Demigod named the First Dragon," Aisling corrected herself. "Do you guys have a First Vampire?"

"Not quite. Christian would be the one to ask about specifics—since not only was he around more than a thousand years ago; he is very hip with all the lore—but from what I remember, there were four kings. Not mortals, but some sort of being who had abilities with dark magic. They decided that it was their role to save mankind from the evil of Abaddon, and tried to destroy the demon lord princes."

"I used to be a prince of Abaddon," Aisling said nonchalantly.

I gawked at her. *Holy shit.*

What? Christian looked up at me, his eyes searching the room for a threat. *Did one of the women insult you?*

No. Far from it, they're very nice, although Ysolde keeps eating the food they brought me. Aisling said she used to be a prince of Abaddon.

Christian eyed her. *She doesn't seem to be tainted with the stink of Abaddon. Not even the demon smells bad.*

I know. It's kind of odd. "How on earth did you end up with that job?" I asked.

She waved away the question. "It's a long story. Go on with what you were saying."

"There's not much more, unfortunately. Or rather, there probably is, but I don't know it. The four kings—they were related somehow, but I forget if they were cousins or brothers or what—they tried to take down the princes, and lost. And were cursed into an early form of Dark One."

"That's fascinating," May said, absently scratching the demon dog's belly as it lay on its back, legs kicking in the air.

"Jim, that's unsightly," Aisling said. "And you can speak again if you don't do anything to freak out these nice vampires."

"Oh, yeah, baby, right there," Jim moaned as May scratched its armpits. "I love girls with dragon claws."

May gave a little eye roll, pulled her hand out of its furry black pit to show her hand covered in silver scales, tipped with scarlet curved claws. "Sorry," she told me as her hand rippled for a second, then returned to normal. "I didn't mean to startle you."

"No, no, it's all so fascinating. You guys really have a different form? Vampires are what you see. They don't change appearance at all." I paused for a second, then had to add, "Well, they can look older or younger if they want, but that's it."

"Turnabout is fair play," Aisling said, sitting back. "Do you want to fill her in on dragonkin, Ysolde?"

"Soldy, claw scritches?" Jim asked, still on its back, managing to shimmy its way over to her. "May only did one pit, and you know how it is when you only have one pit satisfied."

"Oh for Pete's sake … go on, Ysolde," Aisling said, bending over to scratch her dog's armpit.

The next ten minutes were eye-opening, and I passed along many of the things she told me to Christian, who didn't comment other than saying that dragons were not nearly so pleasant as they might appear.

"Is this all the food that is left?" he asked a half hour later, having perused the hospitality table. I was still sitting in the chair next to the heating vent, although I was now thoroughly warmed up, and was chatting with May about her life in Australia.

"You are a Dark One," the dragon named Kostya said. He frowned a lot. "You don't eat food."

"No, but my Beloved does, and it would appear that you have left her little to pick from."

I'm fine, Christian. I had some grapes—

That is not enough. You didn't have lunch, and fed me before we left. You need food. I can feel your hunger.

Stop eavesdropping on my belly. Besides, it wouldn't hurt me to lose a couple of pounds.

I am not going to let the dragons eat all your food!

Not going to address the few-pounds comment?

He made a scoffing sound in my head. *You know I find your body beyond desirable just as it is.*

I smiled at him, warmed to the tips of my toes with the few erotic images he sent my way. *Yes, and I love you, too. But maybe lighten up a bit on the dragons. There's more of them than us, so it makes sense they'd eat the bulk of the snacks.*

"We are getting a bit low. Maybe we should go forage?" Aisling said, turning to her husband. "There has to be a storeroom somewhere with food for the VIP lounge."

"We can look. Kostya?"

"I have already been dragged out to do menial chores," he answered, crossing his arms. He plopped himself down and looked stubborn. "Let someone else go. Baltic, for instance."

The dragon named Baltic, who reminded me of Christian for some reason I couldn't put my finger on, ignored the man and continued speaking to the boneless boy Brom.

"Bah. Of course he is *busy*," Kostya said with a snide emphasis on the last word. "Since Baltic is being unreasonable, as usual, then Gabriel can do it."

We looked at where Gabriel sat at Finch's table, chatting with him.

Both men ignored Kostya.

I giggled in Christian's head. He sighed in mine.

"I'll go alone since you are so determined to be an ass," Drake said, and started for the door.

"Fine," Kostya snapped, looking extremely put-upon. "But this is the last time."

"Why don't you go with them?" I suggested to Christian, who looked horrified at the thought.

"I will not leave you unprotected," he said stiffly.

Oh, for heaven's sake. I'm not in danger.

I will not leave you alone with these dragons.

"I'll go," Finch said, giving his uncle a look I couldn't interpret.

The two dragons didn't look any more thrilled with the idea than Finch did, but all three marched resolutely out the door, closing it quietly behind them.

"Do you think we should ration the food?" Aisling asked Ysolde in a quiet tone. "There's plenty of drinks, and of course hot water for tea and coffee, but the snacks are starting to thin out. Jim, so help me god, if you eat one more popcorn bag, I will give you the doggy barf-up medicine."

"You can't," Jim said, sucking its teeth as it sauntered over to plop down next to me.

"Want to try me?" she asked, narrowing her eyes on it.

"Blizzard is here. You aren't going to want to take me out in it to have me ralph up perfectly good buttery popcorn bags, are you?"

We all turned to look at the window. Evidently the windows were extra soundproofed, because we didn't hear the wind, but the fact that the snow was a solid sheet of white moving horizontally told me the demon was right.

"Dammit. All right, I won't make you puke up the bags, but stop eating them. And anything else. I have your food in my bag, so you can have your regular dinner when it's time."

"Aw, man! That stuff sucks behemoth balls. Big ones!" Jim gave me a pathetic look. Despite it being a demon, I couldn't help but pat it on its head. I always was a sucker for a dog. "Ash listens to bad veterinary advice. I bet you have a fine appreciation of just how hard it is to maintain such a fabulous shape, don't you?"

"Well, you are quite fluffy—" I told it.

"Aisling! The vampette says she wouldn't make me eat that ass-flavored diet food if I were her personal demon," the dog shouted.

"That's not what I said—"

"Do you want to go to the Akasha?" Aisling asked in a sweet voice that was threaded with steel. I recognized it as being the ultimate mom voice, the same tone I used with much effect on my girls. "Because I can arrange for that."

"Geesh, some people don't know how to take amusing repartee," Jim said, sticking out its lower lip in what I would call a pout had it been in human form. "When I thought this trip without the spawn meant it would be just like old times, I didn't mean the old times when you starved me by making me eat ass food."

"If you refer to your food—perfectly nutritious dog food, which is incidentally extremely expensive—by the term 'ass' again, you won't get any of the canned food," Aisling told it.

"Demon lords," Jim said, sitting on my foot. "You can't live with them, and you can't live with them. You going to eat that half a scone? 'Cause I'm happy to take care of it for you so you don't have it sitting there on the table next to you, getting in the way of everything."

"It's fine where it is," I said, jerking my foot out from under its big butt before sliding away the sole piece of pastry that had been left to me after Ysolde and Aisling absentmindedly ate their way through the plate of offerings.

"Two of a kind," Jim muttered under its breath, and got up to blight someone else.

About twenty minutes later—while Christian was in the middle of a mental lecture about becoming too chummy with the dragons—the threesome returned bearing assorted small packages.

"Reinforcements!" Aisling said, hurrying over to take the packages from her husband. "Hmm. Just more of the same minus the fresh pastries?"

"The bags of chips, crackers, and nuts were all we could find in the FBO storeroom," Drake told her. "And be thankful we found that. The people stuck in the main terminal saw us, and threatened to break in here to get at what they claimed were our vast resources of food."

"We told them this was all we had, but some mouthy mortal refused to believe us, and was trying to rally the others into breaching our sanctuary," Kostya said, looking indignant.

Oh dear. Shades of mortals storming your castle with pitchforks and torches.

They don't do that anymore. Now it's automatic weapons and spotlights.

"Maybe we should share the food if they are out there without any," Aisling said, looking down at the handful of small packages of chips. "If we tighten our belts for a bit, we could give some to those who needed it."

"There's no need," Finch said, returning to his table and laptop. He tapped on the keyboard a few times to wake up the computer. "I pointed out that there was a row of vending machines that held more items than what we found, and they went off to find something to beat the machines open."

"Oh. Well, then we don't have to feel guilty saving these for us," Aisling said, dumping all the snacks on the table.

"Excellent," Ysolde said, getting up from where she'd been sitting with her husband. "Aisling and I will take over management of the food resources, just so that we don't have any misunderstandings in case the storm runs longer than it's expected."

"And leave my Beloved to starve? I will not have this," Christian said, striding over to eyeball the food that the two women were stacking in wicker display baskets. "If you are forming a food committee, I insist that she be a part of it."

"Oh for the love of …" I got up and punched Christian on the arm hard enough to make him realize just what a boob he was being. "I don't need to be part of the rationing committee. They're not going to withhold food because I'm not one of them."

"You don't know dragons," he said darkly. "They hoard things. That's what makes them dragons."

"He's right, they do," Aisling said, shuffling the popcorn bags to the back after a swift glance at Jim. "But luckily, mates don't usually have that same proclivity. Allie, we'd be delighted to have you join the official food committee. Would you like to be in charge of the chocolate? It's much better that you keep it away from me, since it is one of my biggest weaknesses."

"One of?" Jim asked, but quickly lowered its head to where it was evidently reading a magazine at a gimlet look from Aisling.

The dog reads magazines.

It's not a dog. And stop thinking thoughts about how I'm being unreasonable, and embarrassing you. There is nothing to be embarrassed about a Dark One protecting his Beloved.

There is when there's no reason for the vamp to be so suspicious and prickly. You have the nicest manners of any man I know, and yet all you've been to these people is obnoxious.

If I am, it is to set boundaries with them, and let the wyverns know I will not allow them to dominate us. You will notice they have us outnumbered.

We're not going to fight them, so it doesn't matter. "I'm happy to be the chocolate wrangler, although I don't know that I'm any too strong against its silent, sweet lure," I told the ladies, and helped them finish arranging things. We set out plates for people to pick up as needed, counted packets of tea, cocoa, and coffee, and refreshed the hot water.

It was then that I heard Kostya tell Drake, "We should barricade the doors."

"What? Why?" Aisling asked, passing me with a plate for her husband.

"The mortals might make good their threat to break in and steal our food," Kostya said, scanning the room, no doubt for means to barricade it. "If we had the key, we could simply lock it, but I have searched the desk and there was none."

"I suppose that isn't a bad idea," Drake agreed.

"Of course it's a bad idea. What if the people out there can't get food from the vending machines? We can share if that's the case," Ysolde pointed out, two plates in her hand, one of which she gave to her son, the other to her husband.

"No barricading," Aisling said. "Although ... did anyone think to check the toilet paper supplies? We wouldn't want to be caught short."

"You can't have my magazine," Jim said, trying hard to not let Aisling see it was chewing on a piece of scone that May had slipped it. "It's the Beach Day issue of *Welsh Corgi Fancier*, and that's worth its weight in gold. Oooh, baby, that's it, frolic in the sand for Daddy."

"No, but I have to ... I'll check with you," May said, following Aisling to the bathroom.

"You are the oddest demon I've ever seen," I told the dog.

It waggled its eyebrows at me. "Yeah, but I grow on people."

I wasn't overly worried about anyone trying to break in to get at the food, but I ate the rest of my scone and a few salty snacks so that I could feed Christian later.

How and when Finch would eat was something that we could address when the time came. I figured he'd be fine for a least a day before the situation got dire.

The apprentice Stella chatted for a bit about how excited she was to be with Aisling, who I gathered was some sort of a big noise in the Guardian world.

"It's a coup to have her as a mentor," she said, her tone hushed when Aisling and May returned. "My aunts will be interested when I tell them. Two of them work with dragons, too, but none of them have a Guardian mentor who is also a demon lord. Although my Aunt Sasha—" She stopped.

"What about her?" I asked out of politeness, only half listening to her chatter.

"She has a different sort of job," she said in a tone that caught my attention, but she got up and returned to the big leather couch before I could ask her more.

You're not doing what I think you're doing with that, I said a short while later when Christian emerged from the men's room with a small wooden wedge, no doubt used to keep the door open when the bathroom was being cleaned.

Of course I am. I don't want mortals storming in here any more than the dragons do.

I gave him a mental eye roll, but since I also didn't think anyone was going to starve over the few hours we'd be grounded, I said nothing when he slid the wedge under the door leading out to the main terminal.

The dragons saw, however, and gave him curt nods of approval.

"We are go on toilet paper, I'm happy to say," Aisling announced. "So feel free to use it as needed. Well. Here we all are, snug as can be despite the blizzard going bonkers outside. All things being equal, we're not in a terrible situation, are we? We have food, shelter, warmth—"

The ceiling lights flickered three times, dimmed, then went out with a buzzing noise. Blackness enveloped the room, the only light coming from outside, where the wind was flinging the blizzard at the windows.

"Way to go, Ash. Now you cursed the lights," Jim's voice said from the depths of the darkness.

Allegra?

I'm fine. Where's my phone …

Several small patches of lights suddenly illuminated strained faces as everyone else had the same idea, turning on their phone flashlight function.

"Well, crapbeans," Aisling said, holding her phone up to shine it around the room. "That was unfortunate timing. I don't suppose you guys saw any camping equipment while you were out foraging for food?"

"Camping equipment?" Finch asked, closing his laptop. It had remained on when the power went out, but I suspected he didn't want to wear out the battery.

"Lanterns," she explained, turning the light onto him. "Maybe sleeping bags if it gets cold. Or better yet, a generator? Maybe the airport people have an emergency backup generator? Are there any employees still left here, or are they all over at the hotel?"

Drake sighed, and got to his feet. "I did not see a generator or camping supplies, but it wouldn't hurt to search the premises again. Kostya?"

"No." I couldn't see his face, but the annoyance fairly dripped from his voice. "Let someone else go out there. Besides, we have strangers here. Someone has to protect the mates."

"Oh, you did not just call us helpless," Aisling said, and in the faint glow from the phone Ysolde held up,

I could see the look all three women gave the grumpy dragon.

He flinched.

"Not to mention the fact that vampires normally have excellent manners, and wouldn't dream of attacking anyone unless they were being threatened," I said with a little frown at Kostya.

He sighed heavily, and got up, but grabbed the silver-eyed Gabriel as he did so.

"If you are going to make a servant of me, then Gabriel should come along, too."

"Why?" Gabriel asked after shaking his arm free of Kostya.

"It's only right, given that you should be a black dragon."

"Oh, for the love of god—please, don't get that started again," Aisling said, and the other dragon women muttered agreements.

"Touch me again, and you'll find your collarbone smashed to smithereens, and I will *not* heal it," Gabriel said in a pleasant tone as he stalked forward, following Drake.

Just as the latter reached the door, pounding filled the room, making me jump at the same time several others exclaimed.

"It's the mortals!" Jim said, backing up. "They've come for our food! Protect it at all costs! Roast 'em alive, Drake."

The dragons stood for a moment at the door, all three of them with heads cocked as if they were listening; then Drake bent and removed the door block, whipping open the door.

A blast of cold air entered the room with the three people who followed it.

"Now anyone who wants is coming in?" Kostya asked, gesturing at the newcomers. "This is our lounge! We claimed it first. You must leave."

"Like hell we're going to do that. There's a war going on out there over some vending machine snacks," the first of two women said, rubbing her arms as she glanced around. It was hard to see her face clearly, since she didn't have a phone giving her light, but the woman behind her did, as did the large man behind them both. "Oh good, you're not mortals. I thought we'd have to hide in the bathroom, since Pixie's glamour is going to fade any second, and I really don't want that crowd to see her without it. Er ... this *is* the private-plane lounge, yes? We were told we could hire one to get us to Seattle, since our flight was diverted due to weather, leaving everyone stranded in Ottawa."

"Yup, this is the VIP lounge. Oooh, polters," Jim said, having moved unseen in the darkness to sniff the newcomers' legs. "Haven't seen any of you guys in a while."

The first woman stared in stark surprise at the dog. I knew just how she felt. "That's Jim. It's a demon, but evidently quite nice," I told the woman, then held out my hand. "I'm Allie. This is Christian, my husband, and Finch over there is his nephew. They're Dark Ones."

"And dragons, if I'm not mistaken," the big man said, moving to the side of the first woman. Even in the dim light, I could see he had very pale blue eyes. "Name's Adam Dirgesinger. This is Karma Marx, and her ward, Pixie O'Hara."

"Why don't we just open the door and let everyone come in?" Kostya said, waving his hands about in a dramatic fashion. "Maybe I should make an announcement on the loudspeaker system alerting all the mortals to the existence of the lounge? Paint signs with arrows pointing here? Do an interpretive dance?"

"Is that four or five drinks we're up to?" I heard May ask Aisling.

"Six," Ysolde answered, then came forward with several cups of tea. "Drink up while we still have hot water."

HOUR THREE
KARMA

"Aisling! How nice to see you again." I smiled as the woman Pixie and I had met in Paris bustled over to us. "And Drake, too."

The latter bowed. Adam shot me an odd look, as did a couple of the others.

"We met Karma and Pixie at G&T a few months ago," Aisling said by way of explanation. "You both look well. How was your train ride?"

"Eventful," I said as Pixie gave a short bark of laughter.

"Oh? Well, you can tell me all about it, but first, let me introduce everyone," Aisling said, and waved a hand at the gathered people.

It took some time before all the introductions were made, but at last we had claimed one of the tables that was apparently unused. I peeled off my coat while Adam hauled over two chairs for Pixie and me just as her glamour wore off.

"Cool," the demon dog apparently named Jim said as it sat down next to Pixie. "You got the full four arms, huh?"

"You don't look like a demon," she said, wriggling her extra set of arms. "How come you're not in Abaddon? Do you do evil things? What is your demon lord's name? Can I make you do things? How many people have you tormented?"

"I like you," Jim said. "You ask good questions. You want the story of my life? Settle in, sister, because it's a long one. It's been particularly hairy the last ten years or so since Aisling became my demon lord. You wouldn't believe the stuff she's made me do."

"I'm going to look for lights or a generator," Drake said, heading for the door.

"I'll come with you." The man named Gabriel followed, although he didn't look any too pleased with the idea.

"There's no need," Christian Dante said, casting a look at the dragon that made me feel twitchy. "I wouldn't want it said that the Dark Ones shirked their duty. I will assist in the search."

I glanced at Adam. He cocked an eyebrow at me. "Should we help, too?" I asked him in a whisper.

"You? No. But I suppose I should, since our reception wasn't the best, and it would look good for Team Polter to contribute to the group well-being."

"Good point. I'll go with you—"

"Stay with Pixie," he said softly enough that she didn't hear, involved as she was with grilling the demon Jim.

"Gotta go walkies," Jim said, abandoning Pixie to follow Adam when he went to join the other two men.

"Jim, there is a blizzard going on right now," Aisling called across to it. She'd set up her phone at the table containing some food, and was making cups of tea and cocoa. "I don't want you going outside. You'll get lost, and then I'll have to go out and find you."

"Can't it … you know … use a toilet?" Pixie asked. "It is a demon, after all."

Before the dog could answer, Aisling said, "Yes, but Jim's aim is terrible. With its leg cocked up, it can't see where its … er … it can't utilize a toilet without a mess."

"Yeah, the last time Aisling ordered me to use a urinal, she had to pay for dry cleaning on three guys' pants," Jim said with a rusty heh-heh-heh laugh.

"We just gave up trying to get it to use proper facilities," she agreed, then asked the demon, "Can't you hold it for a bit? The storm has to pass at some point."

"No, I gotta go!" The demon tipped its head and bobbled its little eyebrows.

"I can't believe I'm going to say this—go inside," Aisling said with a gesture of general defeat. "Just make a note of where you go so I can tell the airport to clean there later. And don't do it around anyone. Or on carpet. Find a place where there's tile or linoleum or something easy to clean up. And no pooping!"

"See?" Jim said, casting a look back at Pixie, who was taking notes in the journal she'd picked up in Istanbul. "My life is one long adventure. *Hasta la vista,* babies!"

"Be careful," I mouthed to Adam when he followed the other two men as they left our sanctuary. He lifted a hand in acknowledgment, and was swallowed up immediately by the blackness that filled the main terminal.

"So, poltergeists," Aisling said, coming over to our table with two more cups of tea. She sat down in Adam's chair, smiling at us both. "We didn't get a chance to talk about this when we first met, but I have no idea about your people. I always thought you were the spooky ghosts who lived in TVs, and threw things around rooms."

"Deus," Pixie said, rolling her eyes and getting up to move across the room next to the window, where a young man who'd been introduced as one of the dragons had draped himself over the chair.

"Sorry about that. She's a bit … well … sixteen," I said, gesturing vaguely.

Aisling laughed. "No worries. My twins are nine, and I'm already dreading their teen years. They're such terrors now, I can't even imagine what hell awaits us."

"That's what wine is for," Ysolde said, followed by the woman who looked like she'd stepped straight out of a 1920s silent movie. They dragged with them a small love seat, collapsing on it with a shared giggle.

"Are we talking kids again?" Allie joined us, frowned, then hauled a free chair over and wedged it in beside me. "Josef—he's our oldest—kept trying to stake Christian until he was four. Josef, not Christian. The girls are convinced they can fly if they focus hard enough. I can't tell you how grateful I am that they're Moravian and thus immortal, because otherwise Christian would cocoon them in Bubble Wrap until they are eighteen."

"My son likes to mummify dead animals," Ysolde announced, nodding at the person in question. We all looked, and I found myself staring with astonishment as Pixie, all four hands gesturing, talked with the young man named Brom. He leaned against the window and periodically nodded, his arms crossed, but his body language expressing focus on what Pixie was saying.

"Well, now," Aisling said, glancing back at us with a twinkle in her eye. "That's interesting. Brom's what … eighteen now, Ysolde?"

"Yes." She made a face, then gave a short laugh. "And up to this point, aside from one date earlier in the year, hasn't been the least bit interested in girls. Or boys, for that matter."

"Karma was just going to tell us about poltergeists," Aisling said, sipping at her tea. "Ugh. It's getting cold. Drink up, ladies."

"Maybe the others would like some," I said, nodding toward the nearest dragon, Gabriel. The woman introduced as Stella was chatting with him but, at a look from May, hurried over to join us, squeezing in beside Aisling with a murmur of apology.

"Eh. Most of the men prefer things other than tea," Aisling replied. "Ow. That was my hand you squished with the chair, Stella."

"My apologies. I'm just so excited. First dragons, then Dark Ones, and now poltergeists. It's a red-letter day for me!"

"She takes notes," Aisling told me when Stella pulled out a tablet and looked expectantly at me.

"Er … OK. I'm not sure I have anything to say that's particularly noteworthy, but I'll try to be as pithy as possible."

"What is he doing—oh good." Ysolde, who had been craning her head when Kostya emerged from the bathroom, settled back when he returned to his seat at the window. "So long as Baltic stays where he is, everything should be OK."

The second she said the words, the object of her attention rose, his eyes narrowed as he dragged his chair over to sit next to her. "I dislike it when you speak of me as if I am a problem," he told her. "I am the most peaceful of dragons."

May and Aisling both choked, Aisling to the point where May had to pound her back.

Baltic ignored them.

"Considering that the entire weyr sentenced you to death, that statement doesn't really hold up," Ysolde said, but she took his hand in hers, and sent him a look that had his eyebrows rising. "And Karma, before you ask, yes, Kostya and Gabriel are at odds with Baltic. I won't go into the history of why, but you can take it as read that they tend to argue when they get together, so we've found it best to keep them separate as much as possible."

"I am not to blame if the other wyverns have no ability to control themselves," Baltic said, shooting a potent glance at Kostya.

"Are you speaking ill of me?" Kostya asked, leaping to his feet.

"I was simply pointing out that you have no control," Baltic said, looking bored.

"Oh, lord," Aisling said, her shoulders slumping as Kostya stomped over to us.

Stella gave an excited squeak and tapped madly on her tablet.

"Me? You say that of me?" Kostya's voice rose. "*You*, who are responsible for the death of so many black dragons, you say that of *me*?"

"Just so you know, poltergeist, he smote me in two the second I lowered my sword," Baltic told me, now looking self-righteous.

"Because you were killing our kin!" Kostya snapped, his hands waving.

"And this is why we try to keep them apart," May said sotto voce.

"I didn't kill our kin." Baltic gestured toward where Gabriel was still reading a book, although I noticed he hadn't turned a page in a while. "You can thank the silver dragons for that."

"We did nothing but try to save our sept from your murderous ways," Gabriel said, not looking up, but his jaw was tense.

Finch, who had been writing in a small notebook, watched the dragons warily, occasionally glancing over toward us. Allie smiled in what I thought of as a reassuring manner. I assumed that meant she was no stranger to men who were gripped with strong emotions.

"I don't know which of you is more insane," Kostya said, spreading his glare between Baltic and Gabriel.

"Sit down, Kostya," Aisling said, giving him a little push, which he reacted to by moving his glare down to her. "We're not going to let you pick a fight in front of our new friends. Although …" She waited until Kostya retreated to the far end of the room. "Although we might have to let the guys work off their bad moods soon."

I had no idea what she meant by that, but decided it must be a dragon thing.

Baltic's expression brightened, but before he could say anything, Ysolde said, "Go ahead, Karma. We interrupted you when you were going to fill us in on poltergeists."

"I don't know how much there is to tell. We're not really that exciting," I said. "We're not ghosts, as popular lore would have it. In fact, we're really no different from vampires and dragons in that polters are also a unique race of beings—although demon lords can curse mortals to that state."

"They can do that with vamps, too," Allie said. "We know of one guy who was a fallen angel, and a big bad demon lord zapped him into vampiness."

"Bet it was Bael," Aisling said, making a face. "Sounds like the sort of thing he loved to do. He's out of commission now, fortunately."

I thought for a minute. "We have a language called Poltern that is a little odd, and fanned the flames of the spiritualism craze of the Victorian era."

"How so?" May asked.

"The language is made up of knocks and clicks made by popping toe joints," I said in Poltern.

Astonishment graced all their faces for a few seconds, before I repeated the sentence in English.

Aisling set down her cup of lukewarm tea. "The dragons have their own language, too, but it's just a language, not noises. How did your language bring on spiritualism? I have a vague memory of that being started by some sisters in the US."

"The Fox sisters, yes, but they later admitted to being a fraud. Actually, the source was mostly due to the Civil War, and the loss of so many family members. People were desperate to get in touch with their loved ones, so the spiritualism craze spawned. Later, when World War One was raging, the Spanish flu hit and between the two, millions died. That was the second push of spiritualism. Our language of what sounds like mysterious raps and knocks, and the fact that polters drop apports—little stones—more or less formed a basis of all things ghostly that mortals tied into their concept of spiritualism."

"And you have multiple arms?" Allie asked, glancing at where Pixie was now showing Brom something on her phone, their heads close together as they looked at the screen.

I made a mental note to schedule Pixie an appointment with a local polter doctor for a discussion of birth control options. Not that I expected her to have an immediate need for it, but her reaction to the young man drove home the point that she wasn't the child she sometimes appeared to be. "Yes, some polters are born with four arms, and lose the extras over time. Those who haven't, like Pixie, use glamours to get around in public, but unfortunately, she used up hers while we were visiting my mother in Quebec. Unfortunately, there were none available there, and now we're on our way home, and haven't had time to get her more."

"This is sucktastic," Pixie said, appearing suddenly at my shoulder.

May, who was sitting to my left, jumped.

"We can also move very fast when we want to," I told her, then slid a look up at Pixie, who frowned at me. "I agree that being stuck by a blizzard isn't fun, but everyone is making the best of it."

"No, not this." She gestured toward the windows, which also happened to include Brom, who now stood leaning against the glass, an inscrutable expression on his face. "It's almost Christmas Eve, and we're not home with the tree, and presents, and the big Christmas dinner you said I could make."

"Pixie has recently discovered a love of gourmet cooking," I said with what I hoped would be a daunting look at her, but she just rolled her eyes and slumped down onto the floor next to me. "I'm sorry that we're not home to enjoy the tree and presents, but both will be there when we get back."

"Tree," Aisling said, turning around in her chair to stare at the tree in the corner of the lounge.

"Presents," Ysolde said in the same speculative tone of voice.

"That's an excellent idea," Allie said, nodding at Pixie. "I have a few things in my luggage—"

"And I have some things I picked up for the kids, but they won't miss them. You wouldn't believe what

Drake thinks is a suitable number of presents for children," Aisling said, getting to her feet.

"We have champagne, but Baltic can just survive the loss of a little Bolly to bolster everyone's spirits. I assume those presents under the tree are just wrapped empty boxes?" Ysolde asked.

"Mate, you go too far," Baltic protested, glowering at his wife. "I am a reasonable dragon—"

All three mates just looked at him.

"—but I draw the line at sharing my good champagne with those who until recently not only sought my own death, but yours, as well."

"I feel like you've got a hell of a story behind you," I told Ysolde.

"You have no idea," she said, standing up. "Shall those of us who wish to fill a few of the empty present boxes divide them up, and go to our corners to do a little covert wrapping?"

"*Chérie*," Baltic said, his voice suddenly persuasive and smooth, "I understand your need to be generous, but about this, you are being unreasonable—" He followed her over to the tree, obviously trying to talk her out of her plan to dole out his champagne.

"I'm happy to join," I said, thinking about the few things I'd picked up in the arts and crafts consignment shop my mother ran benefiting a local charity. I had planned to save the items as incentives for Pixie during the upcoming year, but I'd find local substitutes once I got home.

We broke up after a little more discussion—and agreed that no expensive items would be included, the Bollinger champagne aside.

"I'll take these three boxes," I told Pixie. "And I can do one on your behalf and one on Adam's."

"I can do my own," she said, taking two colorfully wrapped boxes the size of large mugs. To my surprise, she shouldered her bag, and moved over to where Brom was sitting cross-legged on the floor, plopping down next to him with her boxes. She obviously explained what she was doing, which led to him getting up and going over to his luggage, then to his mother, who handed him two of her stash of boxes with a surprised lift of her eyebrows.

The other ladies caught the interaction, and all gave me wide-eyed looks. I shrugged, smiled, and gave a little shake of my head before tackling unwrapping the empty boxes without damaging the paper and ribbons.

It took about twenty minutes before the stack of presents was replaced under the tree, but I was pleased to have donated the amethyst runestones, Gothy planner, and old edition of Poe's poems that I'd found in my mother's shop. I had no idea what Pixie had added to her boxes, but was proud that she chose to join in. It had been a difficult year for her, and I was worried that the holiday would be doubly so.

"Getting presents is always nice," I told her when she returned to curl up in a chair next to me. "But there's something really gratifying about waiting for someone to open up a present you like."

"I guess." She tried to look grumpy, but a smile curled her lips as she leaned close to whisper, "I just hope whoever gets mine likes Swedish death metal."

Adam and the others returned before I could even speculate on the likelihood of anyone but one specific eighteen-year-old liking such a thing. Adam held a small lantern in front of him, along with two trash bags.

"We found a stash of emergency equipment behind the airport manager's office," he said, dumping the bags on the floor. "We left some lights with the mortals out in the terminal, along with the bulk of the clothing we took from the lost and found. There were no blankets, but I did collect a few coats in case they're needed."

"Oh, nice. That should perk up everyone's spirits," Aisling said, taking the lanterns her husband held. There were five in total, which she spread around to provide pools of blue-white light surrounded by blackness.

"Man, it's like Abaddon on earth out there," Jim said, wandering over to where I sat with Ysolde and Allie.

"Are they starving? Freezing?" Ysolde asked, her brow puckering.

"Naw. Drunk. One of the guys, a big dude wearing a hat that looks like it's made out of an entire beaver, picked the lock on the door to the bar, and when we came through with supplies, they were doing some weird slinky avant-garde Canadian-Latin dance." Jim gave a shudder. "No one should have to see that sober. It's gonna give me nightmares, I just know it."

"Canadian-Latin slinky dance?" I asked, trying to picture it in my mind.

Fortunately for the sanctity of my own dreams, a disturbance took everyone's attention at that point. I'd been aware that a couple of the dragons were grumbling on the other side of the room, but when Kostya shouldered Baltic aside as he was going over to the food table, Baltic took umbrage with the push.

"Baltic!" Ysolde stood up from where she'd been repacking her luggage.

Her husband had given Kostya a shove in return, causing the latter to stumble over a suitcase and fall into an inelegant heap on a chair.

He leaped to his feet with a snarled, "You put that case there on purpose!"

Baltic crossed his arms. "Why the hell would I do that when you fall over your own feet without my help?"

Kostya snarled an invective in Latin.

"Calm down, both of you," Ysolde said, pulling her husband back a foot. "Baltic, chill. There's no need for you to get riled up trying to teach Kostya manners."

"Ysolde!" Kostya said, outrage evident on his face.

"Oh, get over yourself," she told him, pushing Baltic back another couple of feet.

"She's the only one who can get away with telling the wyverns off," Aisling said softly. "She's the oldest, and knew them all for several hundreds of years before she was killed." Aisling thought for a moment, then added, "The first time. The second time was just a few years ago. Drake, don't you even think of it."

He shot her a look from those wicked green eyes, and marched over to stand next to Kostya.

"Er ..." I was a little worried. Adam, who had been at the window talking with Pixie, glanced at the men, then moved over to stand behind me, his hands on my shoulders in an unmistakable message.

"I think the time has come," Aisling said, looking at May and Ysolde. "Do we have a consensus?"

"I agree," Ysolde said, gesturing at Baltic. His eyes glittered with what I could only describe as an unholy light.

"Mate?" he said, his expression filled with hope.

"Yes. You guys can have a rumble."

"A what?" I asked, a touch of fear skittering up my back as the other dragons gave a cheer. Immediately, all of them removed their jackets and sweaters.

"Oh, excellent! This should be very exciting," Stella said, leaping to her feet so she could pull her duffel bag over to the wall. "I wonder if I should record it? I should, shouldn't I?"

"I know I'm going to," Jim said, marching over to one of Aisling's bags. "I never get to see the beatdowns."

"Dragons get a bit wound up now and again. It's part of their nature," Ysolde said, taking Baltic's jacket and draping it over a wooden chair.

"So we let them beat the stuffing out of each other when the tension gets to be too much," Aisling said, taking her husband's tie and suit coat.

"They explained this to me earlier," Allie said, standing up and dragging the chairs to the edges of the room. The other dragons were doing the same, leaving a large center area. "It's something to do with them being primal and stuff. Luckily, vampires are much more controlled—"

Christian strolled past us, removing his suit coat and a fancy black-and-red waistcoat, tossing both onto the chair next to her.

"Christian?" she asked as he slid off his tie.

He smiled. "It's just bare-knuckle fighting, Allegra. No real damage can be done, and I will admit that there is a strange attraction to the idea of letting off a little steam."

"Oh for the love of—Finch! Not you, too!" Allie exclaimed.

"Dark Ones have just as many passions as dragons," he said, stripped down to just his pants and shirt.

"Wow. And here I was thinking that polters were volatile," I commented, retaking my seat with the other ladies.

"Jim, come sit over here where you're out of the way," Aisling ordered the demon.

"OK," it said in a muffled tone, a cell phone in its mouth. "But I'm filming it for future watching pleasures."

I looked at Adam. He stood next to me, his eyes narrowed on the others.

"Let's see, there's how many … ? Six of you. Seven if we count Adam."

"Please tell me you're not thinking about it," I asked him.

"Adam? Do you want in?" Aisling asked as she settled herself again.

He hesitated a second; then his shoulders slumped. "I'd like to, but unfortunately, I had surgery on my shoulder five days ago, and I wouldn't want to rip the rotor cuff again."

"You guys don't heal up?" May asked.

"We do, but slowly. It takes time to fix hurts," I answered. "Especially since Adam, like me, has some mortal ancestry. Full polters heal faster than we do."

"Six, then. Sounds like we should do teams of two," Ysolde said, taking her seat. "The standard rules apply—no magic, no dragon powers, and, assuming there are vamp powers, none of those, either—fists only."

Aisling opened a bottle of water and poured a little into a small paper bowl for Jim. "And no hitting in any area deemed important for procreation. Some of us might want to have more children."

"Because that's what you need—more spawn," Jim said after setting down the cell phone.

Aisling gave it a look that had it hurriedly drinking the water.

"Kostya, if you gang up on Baltic with more than one person, I reserve the right to box your ears," Ysolde said.

"You wouldn't dare!" he said, looking aghast.

She narrowed her eyes at him.

"Baltic," Kostya said, turning toward him. "Control your mate or I'll be forced to!"

"If you think you can do that, you're welcome to try," Baltic answered. "But it will take a better man than you to do so." He was silent for a moment before adding, "And me, for that matter."

"Yes, but you're the only one who I'll let try." Ysolde blew him a kiss.

Drake and Kostya retired to a corner to speak in low tones, obviously teaming up.

Finch and Christian did likewise.

Gabriel and Baltic looked at each other with mutual dismay. "I suppose we're going to have to set our differences aside," Gabriel said.

"Only if you grant me the right to break Kostya's weak collarbone again," Baltic answered, holding out his hand.

"Agreed," Gabriel answered, shaking it.

"I heard that!" Kostya bellowed across the room.

"This is … I can't believe you ladies are sanctioning this," I said, shaking my head.

"You boys play nice with the new kids," Ysolde told them all, popping open one of Baltic's bottles of champagne and pouring us each a glass of it.

All the men present turned outraged expressions on her. Baltic's was particularly pointed when he noticed the bottle at her side.

May, Aisling, and Allie all giggled.

Brom stood up.

"Absolutely not," Ysolde said. "You're too young."

"Aw, Sullivan," he said in a plaintive tone. I wondered why he called her that, but figured it was a family name. "I'm a dragon now."

"I don't care. You're too young. Baltic, tell him he's too young."

Baltic looked thoughtfully at the boy, then made a face. "He's not too young, but if you insist we have partners, then there is no one for him."

"I'll fight with him," a voice said behind me, and I gawked, absolutely gawked, as Pixie rushed past me, standing next to Brom with a pugnacious expression.

"Oh, hell no," I told her. "Do you have any idea what trouble we'd both be in if the Akashic League found out I let you fight a bunch of dragons and vampires?"

"I'll keep her safe," Brom said with a squaring of his shoulders.

Pixie smacked him on the arm. "Dude! I have four hands. You think I can't take care of myself? Plus, I'm fast."

I leaned slightly to the side and said quietly, "Will the men attack her?"

"Not in the least. She might get a bit jostled around by the hullabaloo, but none of them will so much as lay a finger on her," Aisling said just as softly.

I looked at the others, who nodded their agreement.

"OK, but I'll hold you to that," I said before raising my voice and telling Pixie, "If you get hurt, I don't want to hear any complaints."

"Woot!" she cheered, and grabbed Brom to pull him back for a fast discussion, all four of her hands dancing in the air as she talked.

"I hope to all the gods and goddesses that you are right," I said.

"Don't worry, the men won't touch Pixie, and I'm willing to bet they'll be gentle with Brom," Aisling said.

"Oh, absolutely. Baltic wouldn't let him fight if he truly thought he'd get hurt. Ready?" Ysolde stood up, glancing at her watch. "You can have ten minutes. No breaking any furniture, and remember that anyone who gets hurt has to let Gabriel heal them, and that frequently involves his saliva. Go!"

I don't know what I expected to happen the second she said "go" … maybe that they'd circle around one another, taking the measure of the opposing teams? What happened instead was sheer chaos.

"That's interesting," Adam said, standing next to me, flinching in sympathy when Kostya, with a battle cry that made my ears ring, leaped on Baltic, who would have been fine if Gabriel hadn't swung at Drake and got knocked back into his teammate.

All four men went down in a tangle of arms and legs.

"I am so glad I'm filming this," Stella said, moving to the other side of the room to get a better angle.

Finch and Christian looked at each other, then, with yells, threw themselves onto the pig pile.

Pixie raised her hands as she sent me a plaintive glance.

"Don't look at me," I said, shaking my head. "I'm a pacifist by nature."

"I'm not," she said, and then, with an oath, threw herself onto the back of the nearest man, who turned out to be Finch. He twisted around, his fist pulled back until he realized it was Pixie.

Brom screamed a vulgar phrase in Latin and jumped on Finch, grabbing his hair and jerking him backward so that Pixie rolled free. I noticed she got in a kick on Finch's knee as Brom rolled on the floor with Finch, and at one point, white scales rippled up his arms.

"Brom! No shifting!" Ysolde called, applauding when Baltic and Gabriel, who were once again on their feet, did simultaneous headbutting moves on Drake and Kostya. "Human form only."

"Sorry, I didn't mean to do that," came the breathless apology as Brom released his hold on Finch's neck, shaking his arm until the scales and gold claws dissolved into a normal arm and hand.

"Apology accepted," Finch said, then flung Brom over his head in a move straight out of a Jet Li movie.

"Hey!" Pixie yelled, and flickered past him to where Brom was groggily shaking his head, slumped against the door.

"Wow. You're right—you guys can move fast," Aisling said, giving a low whistle.

"It's a polter trait," Adam said, pumping his fist when Pixie got Brom onto his feet. "We call it flickering. Go for the kneecaps, Pixie!"

"Ahem," I told him.

He pointed at the scrimmage. "They heal faster than we do. A few broken kneecaps are nothing to dragons."

"You want to join us?" Kostya snarled, standing up in the middle of the men, his hair standing on end, and blood seeping out of one nostril.

Adam looked like he was going to take him up on the offer, but I tugged on his hand until his posture relaxed. "Fine, but the next time we're trapped at an airport in the middle of a blizzard with a roomful of vampires and dragons, I get to fight them."

"I doubt if we'll ever be in this situation again, but if so, then you can fight with my full blessing. Er ..." I pursed my lips. "I can't help notice that the dragons now seem to be shirtless."

Finch, Christian, and Brom, who were in a four-way battle with Drake, all paused for a minute, then glanced back at us.

Stella was damn near dancing with happiness as she held up her tablet, focused on the men whose bare chests glistened light off the five camping lanterns.

"Yes, and there's not one single thing wrong with that picture," Aisling said, smiling broadly.

Finch, Christian, and Brom looked at one another. Immediately, three more shirts went flying.

"Not one," Ysolde agreed.

Pixie's eyes widened at the sight of the now-shirtless Brom.

"Don't forget to breathe," I yelled over the noise to her.

She nodded, but didn't take her eyes off Brom's back as he and Christian went into a little boxing routine.

A flutter of cloth caught my attention. The expression on Adam's face dared me to comment on the fact that he had removed his shirt.

"Nice six-pack," Aisling said in approval. "Although I see what you mean about the shoulder. It looks like it's still a bit painful."

"Only when I try to wrestle," Adam replied, crossing his arms, which made *my* eyes widen. It took me a minute to remember my advice to Pixie, but at last I dragged my gaze off the enticing man next to me.

"This Dark One is baring his fangs!" Baltic announced, pointing when Christian pulled back for a punch.

"Christian!" Allie said, holding out her glass for Ysolde, who poured more champagne. "No fangs. You heard the rules."

"It's an automatic response Dark Ones have when we're attacked," the vampire grumbled, but his face twitched a few times until his fangs disappeared. "But I would like to point out that the dragon has his claws out."

Baltic whipped a hand behind his back. "I am a Firstborn. It is normal for our dragon self to be quick to rise to the surface."

"Don't even think of trying that excuse," Ysolde said, holding up the bottle and waggling it at Adam. He quickly offered up his empty glass. "You also know the rules. Five more minutes."

"Why are you all rolling away from me!" Pixie asked, stomping through the middle of the twisting bodies. "I want to kneecap someone!"

"Dear goddess above, this is the best moment of my life," I heard Stella say in a husky voice as she moved around the center circle of action, still filming with her tablet.

"That sort of attitude is going to have me tattling to Dr. Wellbottom the next time you see her," I told Pixie.

She stood in the middle of the roiling bodies, put all four of her hands on her hips, and bellowed, "Deus, Karma! Just tell everyone I have a therapist!"

"Sorry," I said, making yet another mental note to apologize to her later. "This being a foster parent is really difficult. It seems like I'm constantly putting my foot wrong."

"She's a teen," Aisling said, waving away my guilty feelings. "If she is anything like I was at that age, she'll be irritated by you for everything, no matter what you do."

"You're doing your best," Adam said, giving me a reassuring pat on the shoulder. I was momentarily distracted by the sight of his chest so warm and big and tempting next to me, but forced myself to keep my eye on Pixie.

"It's OK, Pixie. I have a therapist, too. Sullivan made me go to him when I became a dragon," Brom told Pixie, ducking when Kostya whirled around with an attempt to land a flying kick on Finch.

Unfortunately, the latter had moved, and the kick grazed Brom's arm. Kostya looked appalled for a second, and helped Brom up from where he'd staggered backward, asking, "Are you hurt?"

"No," Brom panted. He winced when flexing his arm. "Maybe just a little."

Baltic roared an actual roar, and went flying across the heads of the other dragons, slamming Kostya against the wall with a force that made dust trickle down from the ceiling.

"This is so awesome! I want to be your apprentice forever!" Stella yelled across the men to Aisling, whose face momentarily expressed abject horror before she forced it into a weak smile.

"Ouch," Adam said, wincing again when Kostya and Baltic went down.

"I believe that crack you heard was Kostya's collarbone breaking again," May said.

Aisling hiccuped. "Is there more champagne? I'm saving the dragon's blood for afterward."

"I don't see why we shouldn't indulge. The men are keeping themselves warm, and isn't alcohol a form of antifreeze?" Ysolde asked, popping open another bottle of Bollinger.

"For the love of the saints, woman! That's 1983 La Grande Année Brut. It's eight hundred dollars a bottle, and you're guzzling it with my enemies?" Baltic snarled at her, having just gotten to his feet. He listed heavily to the left side, but almost immediately went down again when Drake threw himself forward onto him.

"No one here is your enemy except possibly Kostya, and I won't let him have any if you prefer," she told the pile of dragons and vampires that immediately formed on top of him. In what I felt was a heroic act, Baltic erupted from beneath them, scattering everyone. "Two-minute warning, boys and Pixie."

"Why don't I get any of the expensive champagne—" Kostya started to ask, but ended yelling, "That was my chest hair!" when Gabriel was knocked forward onto him by a flying leap from Finch.

Gabriel kicked out, and Kostya dropped on top of him, both men grunting in pain.

Pixie danced around trying to find some unguarded knees to attack, but fortunately, not only were the women right and the men obviously took care to watch her and make sure she wasn't harmed; they also ensured their knees were out of range just before she aimed kicks.

"I wouldn't mind a glass," Jim told Ysolde.

Another roar emerged from the dragons still duking it out.

"I take that as an objection to giving you Bollinger," Ysolde answered. "Plus, it's probably lethal for dogs."

"Nuh-uh. Ash?"

"I don't think it is, but it can't be good for you," she answered, sipping appreciatively at her glass.

"Man." Jim flopped down at her feet. "I can't eat greasy popcorn wrappers. I can't eat the carrot cake muffins because they have raisins. And now I can't even have a sip of bubbly. Everyone wants me to perish away to nothing."

"May, would you do the honors?" Ysolde asked.

"Sure." May stood up, weaved a little, giggled, and set down her glass.

Aisling bent down and poured a little bit of champagne into the paper bowl. Jim shot her a grateful look, and slurped it happily.

Stella had moved back around toward us, and I caught her filming Adam. I leaned toward her to whisper, "He's taken."

"Is he?" she asked, not stopping the filming.

I smiled, and let myself flicker at her.

She strangled a scream and leaped backward, moving away quickly to the non-polter end of the line of chairs.

"Trouble?" Adam asked quietly, still watching the men.

"Just letting the apprentice know my staim was claked."

He turned to look down at me. "You what?"

It was my turn to giggle, and I am so *not* a giggler. "Think I'm a little tipsy. Claim was staked."

"Ah." His eyes danced with amusement and passion, but like me, he realized it was folly to pursue that at the moment, and returned to watching the fight. It was now more or less a free-for-all, with the team bonds having evidently disintegrated in the countdown.

May put two fingers in her mouth, and blew an eardrum-piercing whistle.

Only two people were standing—Pixie and Finch, the latter of whom was holding one side, and bleeding from both his mouth and a spot above his eyebrow. The rest of the men had all collapsed onto the ground, panting and making little groaning noises as they tried to move.

"Now what?" I asked when Pixie picked her way over the body-strewn battleground to stand over Brom.

Ysolde set down her glass, and stood. "Now we patch them up."

HOUR FOUR
YSOLDE

"I hope you're pleased with yourself. You have broken your nose. *Again.* This makes, what, three broken noses?" I dabbed at the blood dripping from Baltic's nose. He tried to glare at me, but since one of his eyes was swollen shut, it had less effect than I knew he hoped for.

"Four," he said nasally. "Did the green mate say there was dragon's blood?"

"One bottle is out and the second one is coming," Aisling said, kneeling at one of her pieces of luggage. "There are only two bottles left, but that should be enough to get everyone back on their respective feet. Oh, sorry, sweetie. I thought the pillow barricade would hold you. Would someone mind picking Drake up off the floor?"

"I feel like Florence Nightingale patching up soldiers in the Crimean War," Karma said as she moved through the debris of dragons and vampires, only about half of whom had made it to furniture. She held a bottle in one hand, and a stack of paper cups in the other. "Wine, Christian?"

"No, thank you," he said, groaning when Allie poured him into a chair.

"He only drinks me," the latter answered, then gave a little titter. "Sorry, that came out risqué. I meant he can only feed from me. I'll take a glass, though."

"Oh." Karma looked down at the bottle. "Aisling told me to only let dragons have it. I figured Christian might be able to handle it, but I'm not sure about you."

"It's very potent. Lethal to mortals," Aisling answered, peeling a protectively wrapped sweater off a second bottle before she got to her feet. "Although it might be OK for female vamps? I don't know."

"Neither do I," Allie said, and tried to help Christian put his arm through his shirtsleeve, but he yelped and clutched his arm to his chest.

"There's more Bolly," I told her, ignoring the oath Baltic uttered under his breath. His phone pinged, and he flailed with one arm to try to reach it, but I hopped over his legs and got to it first, taking it over to him, sitting on the arm of the chair so he could see the screen. "It's from Pavel—oh. Ratsbane. No news. They've had the midwife in again, and she says the baby simply isn't ready to be born yet." I propped the phone up on a pillow so he could use it with his uninjured arm.

"I was the same way with the twins," Aisling called from where she was opening the second bottle of dragon's blood wine. "Took me forever to have them. Drake almost had an aneurysm waiting."

Adam, with a grunt of pain, got Drake back onto the love seat from which he'd slid off. His head was bloodied, and one hand was swollen and red, but he didn't look too hurt to me.

"You deliberately waited until Baltic was bringing the house down upon us before you had them," Drake said, trying to raise himself up enough to see Baltic, but the back of the love seat was too much for him, and he collapsed back down onto it with a groan.

"Gabriel, when you're done with Brom's rib, would you mind setting Baltic's nose and taking a look at his arm?" I asked, eyeing my son. He lay on his side on the floor, his eyes screwed up tight as Gabriel knelt next to him. He had both hands on Brom's chest, and wore an abstracted expression that was marred by the blood that ran from his mouth.

"Found your tooth, Gabriel!" May said, holding up a gory object. "Do we want to pack it on ice, or should we just figure you'll get it replaced like the others you've lost in fights with the wyverns?"

May grinned at the sharp look he shot her. Since they were almost—but not quite—as madly in love as Baltic and I were, I knew the look was one based on mutual respect and affection. Heaven knew I received enough similar ones from the love of my life.

"All four of Drake's front teeth are replacements, thanks to these little steam-letting events," Aisling said, stepping over where Kostya lay groaning on the floor.

"Baltic has only lost one," I said proudly, smiling at him.

His brows pulled down in response, his one good eye glaring at me balefully. "Is Brom hurt?"

I leaned down to whisper, "I looked before May got Gabriel off the floor. I think he's just bruised—both his ribs and his pride."

"He fought well, but I will have to increase his training now that he's had a few weeks to get used to being a dragon." He closed his eye, relaxing as I folded up a hoodie and gently eased it behind his shoulder. "What do you think of the girl?"

"I think that's something we will worry about later. They're both young, and they only just met. Here, take a sip of this."

He grunted in pain as I held the cup of wine up to his mouth. Although his lower lip was bloody and swollen, the bleeding had already stopped, and I knew the swelling would start to go down as his healing processes kicked into high. "That means nothing. I knew I wanted you the second I saw you."

"Ha. You wanted to kill me because I was a silver dragon." I smiled down at him, so full of love that for a minute, I could do nothing but count my blessings that after centuries of sorrow and separation, we had finally found each other again. Tears pricked behind my eyes when I thought of him living without me after he'd been resurrected. I asked softly, "How did you survive all that time?"

His eyes opened. The swollen one was definitely deflating, and his lovely peat-brown eyes with gold flecks looked confused for a second; then he understood. His eyes closed again, and his face twisted with pain for a few seconds, but I knew it wasn't due to the recent brawl. "I had a plan."

I bent down to kiss him gently on the unhurt side of his mouth. "I have always loved you, and I always will, dead or alive."

"No more death," he said in a grumpy tone that made me smile to myself. "I tire of asking the First Dragon for boons."

"The same goes for you," I told him, straightening up when Gabriel lurched over to us.

"It's as you thought—there were no bones broken," he said, tipping his head toward Brom. "Just a nasty bruise."

"Thank you." I backed up so he could, with as much good grace as he could muster, tend to Baltic, although I thought he set the nose with a bit more gruffness than was called for. He pronounced the arm injury a mild fracture that would heal, and staggered off to a chair, assisted by May.

"Is no one going to tend me?" came the plaintive cry from the floor. "My mate isn't here."

"And I bet Aoife is glad about that," I heard Aisling mutter under her breath, but she managed to get Drake to hold his cup of wine with his uninjured hand, and went to help Kostya.

It took both of us to get him onto a chair, and he bitched nonstop about others ganging up on him until we shut him up by giving him two glasses of wine.

"Can I do anything for you?" I asked the vampire named Finch, where he lay half on, half off a chair.

"No. I'll heal. I may have to go out and find a mortal to help things along, but I'll be all right in time," he answered. I was about to ask him what he meant, when I realized he intended on using one of the mortals as a blood repository.

"Fascinating," I told him, then returned to Baltic when he struggled to sit up, holding his phone to his ear, no doubt checking in with Pavel and Holland.

"Ask them if Anduin is upset we've been delayed," I told him, then went to the refreshment table to see what we had left.

Christian, with Allie supporting him, limped his way to the bathroom when Pixie emerged from it. I assumed they wanted a little alone time, most likely so she could feed him, and made a note to intercept anyone who might head that way until they were finished.

"Think everyone will survive?" Aisling asked me as she poured some dry kibble into a bowl, mixing it with the last of the warm water.

"No doubt. As usual, they are all feeling particularly martyred and full of self-pity, but at least that horrible tension and petty bickering feeling has passed."

"I'm glad. It's so annoying when they get that way." Her gaze met mine, and I read in it the same worry that lurked in the back of my mind. "What do you think is going to happen with them?"

"The tribes?"

"Yes." She opened a can of dog food and scooped some out, looked at the opened can, then with a sigh dumped the dried food and emptied the can into the bowl. "Jim can have only canned food tonight. I wouldn't normally let him have that many calories, but what the hell. It's almost Christmas Eve."

"I think we're going to have to see whether or not Bastian, Archer, and Hunter can rally the tribes together to face Deus and Xavier," I said after a moment's thought on her question. "But I will say this—Baltic is worried."

She stopped smooshing the canned food with a plastic fork, her eyes guarded as she searched my face. "Drake is, as well, but he always is when anything concerns the welfare of the kids and me. But Baltic ... he didn't say anything at the *sárkány*."

"No." I tried to pinpoint my vague suspicions. "I'm not sure that even he knows what bothers him so much about Xavier, but I can feel it in him whenever the subject is brought up."

"Is it something to do with the First Dragon, do you think?" she asked. "Or is it Xavier himself that worries Baltic?"

"Gossip?" May asked, joining us, her voice pitched low, as were ours.

"Just a recognition of a general sense of trouble," Aisling told her. "Ysolde says Baltic is worried, but she doesn't think he knows why."

"Oh, that's not good," May said, her expression turning somber. "Kawaa called Gabriel this morning, and said that something had touched her songline. Something dragon."

"Isn't that normal, though? She was mated to Gabriel's dad. And also, how is she?" I asked.

"She's well other than being a bit disturbed by the songline thing. She sends her love to you all, and asked me to tell you to send more pictures of Anduin and Brom."

"You have the best mother-in-law," Aisling said with a martyred sigh. "Yours never tries to have you offed."

"Speaking of mothers-in-law, I wonder if there is any use in asking Charity what she knows?" May asked. Both women shot questioning looks at me.

I pursed my lips and rearranged several small bags of smoked almonds. "I wouldn't know. At present, she's not speaking to me. Evidently, she took exception to the fact that I called the First Dragon an interfering jerk, and that the day he pulled his head out of his ass where Brom was concerned, I would throw a party to celebrate. She got a bit snippy with me, and I told her that if she was going to throw her support behind an obvious asshat, then she should not expect any Mother's Day cards from us. The First Asshat got all bent out of shape over that and a few other truths I pointed out, and that, of course, meant Baltic came roaring in to my defense, and, well ... you know how the First Dragon goes at Baltic. It was pandemonium. So if you want to know what the First Dragon's snippy mate is thinking, you'll have to ask her directly."

May and Aisling had hands over their respective mouths, shoulders twitching as they obviously held in laughter. May wiped at her eyes as Aisling said, "For the love of Pete, Ysolde! One day you really are going to go too far, and the First Dragon will snap."

"Eh," I said, shrugging one shoulder. "He loves Baltic too much, even if he doesn't like to show it. Plus, now he has Brom in his sights to groom into wyvern-hood. Goddess help him."

"But Brom doesn't have a mortal parent—oh." May stopped, her face somewhat confused. "Rowan?"

"Yes. The 'one mortal parent' rule doesn't apply when the First Interfering One bops you on the head and makes you a dragon. I gather it's only slightly less potent than being a Firstborn."

"You dragons really do heal up fast—oh, sorry, are we interrupting?" Allie—who had evidently emerged from the bathroom while my attention was elsewhere—came over with Karma.

"No, just a little in-laws talk," Aisling answered, looking over her shoulder to where the dragons were, in fact, all sitting up, although each still had a cup of wine. "Ah. Yes, I see we're past the worst of it. Good. I suppose that since everyone is anxious to be home, we should try to defuse any further outbursts of angst. Maybe we could work up some sort of a Christmas feast, and then open the presents? That should brighten all our spirits."

"Food?" Jim asked, wandering over with Stella in hot pursuit. "I thought you were going to try to starve me in front of everyone."

"Like you'd ever let me forget to give you a meal?" Aisling set the metal dog bowl of canned food on the ground.

Jim curled a lip at it. "Ew. That's—"

"You say 'ass food' one more time, and I swear to all that's demonic, I will donate your presents and stocking contents to a needy dog."

Its eyes got huge. "Jeez, Aisling! You're getting more and more like a proper demon lord every day."

"Eat!" she said, pointing at the bowl.

It picked up the bowl in its teeth and stormed off to a corner, saying indistinctly around the bowl, "I can't believe you'd threaten me with the loss of my stocking and pressies. That's downright demon abuse."

"I'm happy to help distribute food to the men," Stella said, tucking away her tablet. "And in fact ... I was saving this for the flight home ... but no, it's better to share, isn't it?" She pulled out a rumpled bag of licorice allsorts, which she dumped in a paper bowl. The candies looked like someone had sat on them for an extended period of time. "Some extra treats for everyone."

"Oh, how ... thoughtful," Aisling said, giving one of her toothy smiles.

"I almost hate to suggest it, but maybe we should push the tables together?" I said, glancing across the room. "It's not ideal for a group meal, obviously, but it might foster a bit more cheer rather than everyone going to their own little table."

"Good idea." Allie considered the arrangement. "How about if Karma and I get things set up, and we'll let you handle the food?"

"I'm all for a proper feast," Jim said, returning from having consumed its dinner. "I'm not saying I'm going to fall over and die if you don't give me at least one of those cheese Danish, but the likelihood is high, because that dog food you make me eat has no calories in it. And just in case you're worried, I snuffled the Danish really well, and there's nothing in them that I can't have, like onion or garlic."

May, who had picked up a plastic knife and was obviously about to cut up the remaining pastries, stared in horror at the demon. "Wait—did you touch them or just look at them?"

"I'd like to see anyone do a good, thorough snuffle without getting some nose involved. And maybe a bit of lip and some tongue action, just to make sure the ole sniffer is up to par." Jim smacked its lips. "I'm happy to say the cheese Danish are go for dog consumption."

"Well, that's one less item for the feast," Aisling said, scooping up the Danish, and dumping them into one of the empty popcorn bags. "I'd like to have a word with you, Jim!"

"Me?" It squawked when she grabbed it by one of its furry ears and escorted it into the far corner, the demon desperately trying to back away the second she released it.

"Oh dear. Trouble?" Allie asked, watching with a little frown.

"No, just Jim being Jim. Whenever it feels like it's not getting enough attention from Aisling, it pushes boundaries. I think its nose is a little out of joint because Aisling mentioned that she's thinking about having another child. May, what do you think about making a run out to the main terminal to see if there is anything other than chips left?"

She glanced over at where Gabriel was talking to Christian and Finch. "That sounds like an excellent idea."

"Pixie and I can help, if you like," Karma said, having wrestled four of the tables together. "Although it means swaddling her extra arms in a couple of coats and a big shawl that we found in my mother's attic. Pixie? You up to putting on a few extra layers to appear briefly in public?"

Pixie heaved a dramatic sigh, but got to her feet. "I suppose so, but that shawl smells funny, so it had better be a fast trip or I'll start sneezing again."

"It occurs to me that if there's a bar, there has to be a restaurant," I told the exploratory team.

"Yes, but it'll be closed down, and unlike the bar locking up their booze, the restaurant wouldn't be likely to keep food on the premises during the remodel," May protested.

"You say that, but I'm willing to bet you that the staff have somewhere they go to eat, and some sort of food available."

"Makes sense," Karma agreed, and the threesome picked up a lantern and headed out.

We busied ourselves with readying for a feast, and not only assembled a rough approximation of a long dining table but bullied all the men to moving chairs around it, with promises of whatever the expedition could find in the way of sustenance.

"I don't know why you think there is food we couldn't find," Drake said as he strode past me. "We searched everywhere. We're not completely incompetent, you know."

"And the mortals no doubt ate everything in the vending machines," Kostya added. I noticed he still favored one arm, which meant his collarbone wasn't fully healed yet. I thought about punching him on it, but decided that would just end up in another brawl, and the men had already had their fun. "But if you insist on wasting time searching for what is not there, then far be it from us to stop you."

"Aisling, did Drake ever tell you about the time when he was in Madrid, and he posed nude for an academy of female painters?" I made a show of tapping my lip while in abstracted thought. "When was that? Seventeenth century? Sixteenth?"

"Sixteen forty-three," Baltic said, his eyes glinting with humor.

"That's right. We were passing through Spain on our way to North Africa, and we ran into Drake and his harem of painters there."

Aisling turned slowly to look at her husband. "Why, no, Ysolde, he's never mentioned that."

Drake closed his eyes for a moment, then opened them and immediately turned to her. "It wasn't as salacious as Ysolde makes it sound. I was visiting some distant relatives of my mother, and one of them wanted a portrait."

Kostya gave a bark of laughter. "I remember that. Didn't you say that by the time you bedded them all, they started fighting amongst themselves? I seem to recall you saying that you had to leave after the master of the academy found you and the women naked on the studio floor, covered in paint, and indulging in acts for which he threatened to have you gelded."

"Reeeeally," Aisling drawled, her gaze still on Drake.

Jim whistled. "Man, I do love it when Soldy gets annoyed."

Drake didn't even bother to glance my way. He simply took Aisling by the arm and hustled her into a corner, his hands gesticulating madly as he obviously tried to explain.

Kostya gave another laugh. I turned to him. "And speaking of being threatened with gelding, do you ever hear from that druid who swore you dallied with her, and her father tried to get the local lord to have you emasculated unless you paid money for the child? That was about the same time, was it not?"

Kostya squared his shoulders and looked indignant. "It was not my child! Do you think I would father a mortal? She was simply trying to make trouble for me."

"That would be the same druid who you wrote all that endless insipid poetry about, was it not?" Baltic asked, moving next to me.

"Oh, the poetry!" I smiled broadly. "I'd forgotten about that. Didn't you stand beneath her window and recite it every night until she dumped the contents of a chamber pot on your head to get you to stop?"

Kostya leaned forward, his black eyes glittering darkly as he said through his teeth, "I liked it better when you couldn't remember your past."

I smiled, and slid my arms around Baltic, saying nothing. I didn't need to. Kostya kicked aside a chair and threw himself down on the couch, his arms crossed.

"They never learn the folly of crossing you, do they, *chérie*?" Baltic asked softly, his breath tickling my ear.

"You'd think they'd know better by now," I said, turning my head to kiss him. "Did you speak to Anduin?"

"He was asleep. Pavel said that he is quite cheerful, and his only worry is that Father Christmas won't leave us presents if we aren't there in time."

"We'll be there," I told him, and turned when the door opened.

"We return, victorious!" May said, holding up two woolen blobs that turned out to be the sweaters she'd been wearing, now being used as satchels.

"We found the staff room. It had a refrigerator with all sorts of goodies," Karma said, hauling a large sheet of plastic filled with items. "Everything was still cold, so we figure it should be safe to eat."

"Mini-pizzas and grinders and salads," Pixie said, her arms laden with another sweater stuffed full of food packages. "May said the dragons can be microwaves and heat things up for us."

"It took us a bit longer to get back because the mortals are having a full-fledged drunken orgy out there," May said, happily releasing her stuffed sweaters to me.

"Two of them were hooking up," Pixie said, her gaze shifting to Brom, who had fallen asleep sitting in a chair, his head cocked at an uncomfortable angle. "It was, like, so gross."

"Well, you're back now safe and sound," I told them, and we started to unpack items.

Drake did a double take at the food May and company had found, but he said nothing more. I had a feeling he was too busy trying to explain his past.

A half hour later, after pressing Gabriel and Kostya into food-warming duties, we all sat down to the table laden with as much of a feast as we could reasonably expect.

"I feel bad that you and Finch can't partake," I told Christian.

He gestured away my concern, and held a chair for Allie. "It doesn't bother us, I assure you. We're well versed to attending meals we can't eat."

I leaned into Baltic. "Should I offer Finch—"

"No," he said quickly, looking outraged. "There are plenty of mortals he can feed from."

"I hate to be a bad hostess, but I assume he'll tell us if he's in dire need of sustenance. Aisling, do you want to do the honors?"

"—and I don't think sleeping with enough women to be called a harem is 'a minor ripple in your sexual past,' as you insist on referring to it—what?" Aisling straightened up and looked down the table to me.

"I thought you might want to say something festive. Brom and I always had somewhat stark Christmases, so I'm not very good at it." I closed my lips on the subject of his biological father, who was currently residing in a forest in the form of a stone bird.

"Oh, sure." Aisling stood, and cleared her throat. "First of all, I'd like to thank everyone for making this lovely meal possible. May, Karma, and Pixie, you are all champions. Next, I want to say that although it's getting a wee bit chilly here, and we have no power, and no word from the airport people about when we can leave, we have friends, old and new, and a delicious hot meal to dive into. Thank god for dragon fire, eh? Also—" She stopped speaking when her phone started singing a Lady Gaga song. "Huzzah! It's my uncle. Sorry, everyone, I've been trying to get reception for the last few hours. Uncle Damian? Is everything OK with the kids? Oh, thank god. Yes, we're still in Canada—" Aisling and Drake hurried off to the bathroom for privacy.

"I don't think there's anything else to add other than *bon appétit*," I said, reaching for one of the mini-pizzas, which was still steaming.

It was at that moment that the imps attacked.

HOUR FIVE
MAY

"Eeek!" Allie leaped up when the first imps knocked out the grille covering a heating duct and poured out. "What the hell?"

"Imps!" Karma said, also getting up from the table. "Great Northern Imps. Shit!"

"What is a Great Northern—you little bastard! That's my pizza!" Ysolde yelled when one of the imps snatched up the mini-pizza she'd just put on her paper plate.

Gabriel was up in an instant, and instinctively, I shadowed, pulling my daggers out of my leather bodice.

"Why didn't I think to bring a sword with me?" he grumbled as he grabbed the nearest imp, obviously intent on flinging it away, but the imp—which was yellow with black spots, and the approximate size and shape of a full-grown bulldog—snarled and bit into his hand. Gabriel spat out an oath, and breathed fire on the pestilent being.

"Great Northern Imps are notoriously brutal," Karma said, dragging Pixie back from the table while Adam looked around, clearly hunting for a weapon.

"And hard to kill. I don't think your fire is going to do anything to it. Ack!"

The imp Gabriel flung at the wall leaped back at him, teeth flashing. I lunged, my daggers in both hands, but just before I reached him, Gabriel caught me at the waist and spun me around with a hoarse, "No, little bird, do not! They are too dangerous. Don't get close to them."

"I can stab—" I started to protest, but at that moment, another wave of imps came out of the vent, accompanied by two larger green creatures each roughly the size of a small child. "*Agathos daimon!* Boggarts!"

Gabriel swore under his breath while trying to fend off one of the imps, using his body to shield me.

Baltic took one look at the imps, ordered Ysolde behind him, and shifted into dragon form, his white scales reflecting the feeble light of the lanterns in a way that reminded me of a disco ball.

"Like I don't have a dragon form, too?" Ysolde said, and made a face like she was highly constipated. "Dammit! Why can't I shift when I want to? Yes, yes, I'll get behind you, but don't think I'm not going to have something to say to your father later about the fact that I still can't be a dragon when I want to."

"Try breaking their necks," Gabriel called to Baltic and Kostya. "Fire isn't effective."

"Not to mention it risks burning down the airport," Ysolde called from behind Baltic, who was indeed snatching up imps and trying his best to throttle them.

"Where is the one who has defiled our sanctuary?" one of the boggarts asked. It was particularly misshapen, its head hanging between pointy raised shoulders. It jabbed a finger toward me. "Where is the demon, doppelganger?"

"I might have known Jim had something to do—" Kostya, who had also changed into dragon form to fight off three imps, stopped speaking when the imps drew blood.

"Maybe Aisling can do something with them?" I asked Gabriel, reaching around him to stab at an imp that rushed forward. The imps were about knee-high, and basically had everyone backed into corners.

"I doubt if Drake would allow her out if he knew they were here," Gabriel said, grunting in pain when two more imps clamped down on his arm. I had the satisfaction of hearing one of the imps squeal when I stabbed at it, but had a bad feeling that we were at a disadvantage, something that dragons were not used to.

Two forms blurred across the room to a stack of luggage. I didn't have more time to register that Allie was now standing behind Adam with Karma, Pixie, and Stella before there was a flash of silver, and Christian and Finch leaped forward, each bearing a sword.

"What—how do they have those?" I asked, my eyes wide when Christian shouted a battle cry in French and ran forward, lopping off the heads of two of the imps before spinning around and piercing the three attacking Gabriel and me.

"Foresight," Finch called as he headed for Adam and the others, his sword singing as it hacked, swung, and lopped off bits and pieces of imp.

"We never travel without swords," Christian added, kicking an imp to the side before taking off its head.

The two boggarts looked at each other, and turned tail. They oozed their way into the heating vent and disappeared.

It took Christian and Finch three minutes to finish off the imps before the ones that were still coming through the vent took a look at the impy carnage and decided that they had other places to be, and retreated with the boggarts.

Seven minutes after the attack started, Christian and Finch stood panting, their swords and clothing splattered with dark-brown imp blood, the scene one of gruesome horror.

"Jim!" Kostya bellowed, limping his way over to the bathroom. He stayed in dragon form, no doubt to facilitate the healing needed for all the chunks the imps had taken out of him.

"How did you get them through customs?" Gabriel asked Christian, handing him a few paper napkins.

Christian obviously understood the question. "Bribes. Is anyone hurt? Anyone who can't heal themselves?"

"I am, but I refuse to have Gabriel lick me," Kostya said, pausing to examine his arms and one of his rear legs. "Dammit. Like Aoife isn't going to give me hell about my collarbone being broken again, now I'm going to have to explain having a chunk taken out of my calf."

"Well, great," Ysolde said, marching up to where we'd put the tables together. "Just look what they did! They bled on everything and ruined our Christmas feast."

Baltic tore off one of his sleeves and wrapped it around his forearm where a bite freely ran with blood. "Is that all you can think of? I have been wounded, mate!"

"Eh," she said, making a face at the table. "You'll survive. Gabriel can suck your owies if you like. Dammit, not the little sandwiches, too! I was looking forward to them."

"Mate!" Baltic said in an outraged tone until she, with a nasty look at the table, bustled over to attend to him.

"For someone who is the dread wyvern Baltic, he sure is demanding when he gets a hurt," I said softly to Gabriel.

"I am not sucking on any wound," Gabriel told Ysolde, a look of disgust on his face as I took a napkin and dabbed at his own scratches and bites. "Least of all that of Baltic."

"I'm happy to say that all is well back ho—what the hell?" Aisling emerged from the bathroom, Drake and Jim on her heels.

"Abaddon," the demon said automatically, then stopped and looked around the room. "Aw, man! We missed action? I always miss the good stuff!"

"What in the name of sanity has been going on here?" Aisling asked, staring at the pile of imp bodies and body parts that Adam, Christian, and Finch were placing in a tidy stack in the corner of the room.

"Imp attack," I told her, pleased to see that Gabriel's wounds were already closing. I took one of the trash bins and started scraping the tainted food and destroyed presents into it.

"Great Northern Imps, I'm afraid," Karma said, pushing Adam into a chair and grabbing a handful of napkins to tackle the damage he'd gotten protecting them.

"Gabriel?" I asked, nodding toward Adam.

"Hmm? Ah. I doubt he'll appreciate me offering, but I'll try," he said, his beautiful mercurial eyes shining with amusement. He went over to offer his services to Adam, while Ysolde explained to Aisling about the rush of imps.

"It's all Jim's fault," Kostya added, finally back in human form. "They said it desecrated their sanctuary."

Aisling turned on Jim, who tried very hard to look innocent. "Dammit, Jim, what did you do now?"

"Me? Nothing! I mean, I may have peed into a vent because I thought it was better than just going on the floor, but how was I to know that the imps were using it as their temple?"

"For the love of Pete, Jim! You know better than to pee on other beings' things! Didn't the incident with the imp king teach you anything?"

"There was an incident with an imp king?" Karma asked, looking up from where Gabriel was tending to the worst of Adam's wounds with a bit of the silver dragons' healing ointment and a roll of gauze.

"Jim ate it," I told her. "Some years ago. The imps took issue with that."

"I can imagine they did," she said, looking askance at Jim, who, I'm sorry to say, preened itself until Aisling caught sight of it.

"Everything is fine back home?" I asked Aisling a few minutes later when Karma and I had cleared the worst of the mess off the table. Unfortunately, Ysolde was right in that all the food had been destroyed in the battle.

"Yes, other than the kids want us home because we promised them they could open one present on Christmas Eve, which is—" She looked at her watch. "Oh. It's been Christmas Eve for twenty-two minutes. Hopefully the storm will die down enough to let us get out of here in the next few hours, or there's going to be a whole lot of unhappy dragon kids."

"Not to mention insane wyverns," Ysolde said as she walked by with the bottle of dragon's blood, which she was doling out again to all the dragons.

"I didn't think they were hurt that bad," I said softly to Aisling, nodding to where Ysolde splashed a little wine in the cup that Kostya held up.

"I don't think they are," she answered, glancing around the room. "Probably it's more to soothe fractious tempers than anything else. And speaking of fractious, I'd better commandeer a cup of wine for Drake. He's not at all happy that we're missing Christmas with the kids."

The next two hours seemed to pass slowly. Gabriel and I pulled a couple of chairs together, and I curled up into his side with our coats as blankets.

"Not the most ideal of situations," he said murmured into my hair when I snuggled into him, relishing the feel and scent and warmth of him so solid beneath me. "But not one I'm going to complain about in any way. Other than your knee in my balls. If you could move it … thank you."

"I feel bad for the others, though. They have kids waiting for them. We just have Tipene and Maata."

Gabriel chuckled, his arms tightening around me. "You've seen Tipene tear open wrapping paper. I swear he gets more enjoyment from presents than any child."

Christian walked by us, his phone to his ear, speaking in a language I didn't understand.

"True, but I still feel bad for Aisling, Ysolde, and Allie. Oh well, as you say, at least we're together. All of us but Kostya."

Gabriel muttered something in Zilant that I suspect wasn't at all in line with the holiday spirit, but I ignored it.

"Everyone, I'm sorry," Aisling said suddenly, standing on one of the small tables, now smeared with dried imp blood. She held a cup in her hand, and judging by the way she weaved a little back and forth, I figured she had been indulging in either the dragon's blood or Baltic's champagne. "I'm so sorry that Jim ruined the nice dinner that we all worked so hard to steal and heat up with dragon fire. You can rest assured that I have had words with it, and it understands what it has done wrong, and will not do it again."

"Because how many imp sanctuaries are there?" Jim asked from where it lay reading one of its magazines.

Aisling glared at it.

"That is, I swear on the blood of a behemoth I will never, ever pee in a vent of any sort ever again," it corrected, holding up a big black paw.

"I should hope so," Aisling said, then lifted her glass. "Here's to a speedy end of the storm, quick returns to our respective families, and happier days to come."

Several murmurs of agreement followed.

"And it's not like it's all dire," she said, taking Drake's hand when he offered to help her off the table. "We still have the presents to open."

A loud squawk sounded from the corner containing the now-dark Christmas tree and stack of presents, followed by a whumping noise as the tree went up in flames. One of the boggarts ran out from behind the tree, a lighter clutched in its hand, the back of its head on fire as it threw itself into the heating vent.

We all stared at the tree for a second. I sat up on Gabriel to watch in utter disbelief as the tree and the presents beneath all burned merrily.

Everyone in the room turned to look at Aisling.

"Well, *merde!*" she said, slapping her hands on her legs.

"That's it!" Kostya said, stomping over to her. "I forbid you to be cheerful anymore. Every time you do, our situation worsens."

Aisling's jaw worked like she wanted to dispute the charge, but in the end, her shoulders slumped, and she leaned into Drake. "Fine. But I was just trying to make the best of a bad situation. I really want to go home."

"And I will do everything I can to get us there, *kincsem*," Drake told her. "But I would appreciate you not precipitating any other catastrophes until I can do so."

Finch, Brom, and Pixie carried water over to the remains of the tree and the incinerated presents, dumping water on the stinking, smoking mess. They managed to keep the fire from spreading, leaving us with a nasty smell of smoke, and glum spirits to match.

"I have good news," Christian said ten minutes later, returning from where he'd evidently slipped outside, since he was covered in snow. "I managed to get hold of a Weaver. She has agreed to open up portals for everyone, so we can go home."

"Woot!" Aisling yelled, doing a little happy dance.

"Oh, thank the gods!" Ysolde said, applauding him. "You're an MVP, you really are."

"We can go home? Excellent," Karma said, glancing at Pixie, who was standing with Brom, talking with great animation.

I got up, thanking Christian. Gabriel moved in to have a quiet word, no doubt offering financial remuneration for the services of a Weaver, but Christian just gave him a lofty look and a quick shake of his head, which caused Gabriel's dimples to flare when he turned back to me.

A half hour later, everyone had repacked their various garments used to keep warm, and tidied up the room as best as possible. The imp remains had been placed into garbage bags, and we wiped off as much blood and gore as we could.

"The airport isn't going to be happy with us," Aisling said, tying a fresh drool bib onto Jim. "I suppose Drake and I should pay, since it was Jim that made the imps attack, and whatever evil deity is taking my goodwill to mankind and turning it into flaming trees, no power, and a freakin' nonstop blizzard."

The light cast by one of the lanterns began to gather in on itself, twisting and turning until a long dark-purple-and-white tear formed, through which a woman stepped. "Hi! I'm Jenna, and I understand you guys need some portals opened?"

"I've never been so glad to see anyone," Aisling said, taking money from her purse and shoving it at the woman. "London portal shop, please. There will be several of us."

"I'm happy to send you wherever you like—oh, hey, Stella, isn't it? What are you doing here?"

Aisling's new trainee froze when she emerged from the bathroom, her gaze shifting from the Weaver to Aisling, then around the room. "Er ... hello."

"You know each other?" Aisling asked, stepping aside so Drake could toss their luggage into the portal.

"Not really. I portaled her a few hours ago." She named the nearest big town.

"How interesting," Aisling said slowly, turning to face Stella. "Why did you tell me you flew out here if you took a portal?"

"Oh!" Stella slapped a brittle smile on her face and kept her eyes steady on Aisling. "That was a silly conceit, nothing more, certainly nothing important. I didn't want you thinking I was overeager going to the expense of hiring a Weaver."

"Especially as there are three different portal shops in London," Jim said, snuffling her feet. It shook its head, confusion in its eyes when it scooted closer to Aisling.

"Yes, there are," Drake said, closing in on Aisling's other side, pinning Stella back with a look that did not bode well. "Which makes it all that much more curious that you ignored them to engage a Weaver."

Jenna watched us with a wary expression. "Um. I take it something's wrong here. Do you need me to step out for a few minutes?"

"No," Aisling said. "But I would like to know why you lied, Stella."

"And I want to know who you are." Drake took a step forward, and instantly, I felt Gabriel's dragon fire rise in him.

I had a feeling all the dragons heard the note of suspicion in Drake's voice, because they all stopped gathering up their things and moved into a semicircle behind Stella, who was now glancing nervously behind her.

"This is fascinating," I heard Finch say to Christian. "It gives me much insight for my book even if they are dragons. They seem very volatile."

"Dark Ones are just as volatile," Christian insisted.

Finch cocked an eyebrow at him.

"Sometimes," Christian allowed. "When our Beloveds are threatened, we are."

"Granted," Finch said, and turned his gaze back to the scene in front of us.

"Yes, who are you?" Aisling asked, moving to stand beside Drake. "You're not a simple Guardian if you engage Weavers to pop hither and yon."

Stella said nothing for a few seconds, her face working while she obviously tried to think of what to say. "I am as you see, of course," she finally said, holding her hands wide. "I'm sorry that this is such a big deal, but I meant no harm by it."

"Jim?" Aisling narrowed her eyes at Stella.

"Right here, babe," Jim said, a look of happy expectation on its furry face.

"Can you determine if Stella is wearing a glamour?"

"That would be a go from ground control. Demons have the ability to shred glamours if so ordered by their legal and properly endorsed demon lords, of which you have been for the last ten-plus years," it answered.

"Good." Aisling smiled. "Effrijim, I command thee—"

"For the love of the twelve gods!" Stella snarled, backing up until she bumped into Kostya. She spun around, her form shimmering from that of a short, bespectacled brunette to a tall, stately blonde with waist-length hair. She slashed at Kostya with a knife snatched up from the table.

He leaped to the side to avoid being impaled, and instantly, I felt a little stir deep inside, where the dragon heart had touched me, almost taking me over until I'd learned to control it.

"She's not mortal," I said under my breath to Gabriel, goose bumps crawling up my arms at the realization.

"You think you holier-than-thou dragons will stop the Blood Tribe? There is more to them than you know," she snarled.

Gabriel started toward her, but she spat out a word in some language I didn't recognize, and turned, making symbols on the air, then dissolved into nothing before our eyes.

"What—where did she go?" Aisling asked, looking as astonished as I felt.

"To the Beyond, no doubt," Gabriel said.

"The shadow world? Should I go find her?" I asked, pulling out my daggers.

"No. There's no need for that," he answered, tucking away one of them in order to take my hand. "She is not worth the risk."

"I agree," Drake said, looking inscrutable, as he frequently did.

"But why was she here?" Kostya asked. "She was not dragonkin. Why did she mention the Blood Tribe?"

"Xavier," Baltic answered, then helped Ysolde on with her coat. "It matters not. He did not succeed in whatever was his plan in planting her with the green sept."

"No, he didn't, but it's worrisome nonetheless," Aisling said, glancing at me.

"What I want to know is, if she could go into the Beyond, why did she portal here?" Karma asked.

"It was no doubt part of her cover," Drake answered, his expression grim. "Given the expense of summoning a Weaver or even using a portal shop, I assume she felt it would help cement her identity as a simple Guardian. As it is, all she's done is go into the Beyond that touches this part of the mortal plain. She'll have to emerge at some point in order to leave this part of Canada."

"Who's Xavier, if you don't mind me asking?" Allie asked.

"A former dragon who is more or less trying to wipe us out," I answered. "He's rallying some of the ouroboros dragons—ones not in the weyr, as the septs are—to eliminate us. And we don't know why."

Baltic said nothing, although I noticed all the wyverns glanced his way.

"Well, at least this means I won't have an apprentice poking around for the next six months." Aisling gave a feeble smile, then collected her things. "And on that dramatic note, I guess this is where we say *au revoir*."

"One portal to London coming up," Jenna said.

"Me first," Jim said, waiting until Jenna the Weaver opened up another tear. "I want to see the dragons come through. It's always fun to see how wonky they are."

"Yeah, sorry about that. I was told that you guys don't do well with traveling through space. Tuck your hands into your armpits, and take your shoes off," Jenna suggested.

All the luggage went through first, followed by Jim, Aisling, and Drake, the last with a highly martyred expression.

"Wow. Drake's really—" I turned to Gabriel, and saw the exact same expression on his face. "Aww. I'm sure it won't be that bad."

"If it wasn't such a dire situation, I'd wait out the storm," Gabriel answered, his normally bright eyes now dulled.

"Come, my love, I promise I won't let the portal hurt you," Ysolde said as she passed us, dragging an obviously resistant Baltic toward the twisting purple tear.

"You said that last time, and we never did find my trousers," Baltic protested, but heeded Jenna's advice and leaped into the portal shoeless, with his arms crossed tight.

"Is it going to hurt?" Brom asked Gabriel, hesitating when Kostya, with a snarled invective at no one in particular, followed Baltic.

"No, not at all," I told him.

"You'll feel like hell," Gabriel countered, his gaze still on the portal. "It messes with dragonkin on a fundamental level. But it's not deadly. So far."

"Go on, your mom will be there to help you," I told Brom, and held out my hand for his shoes.

Pixie stood on his other side. He glanced at her. She gave him four thumbs-ups. He took a deep breath, and threw himself into the portal.

"Any more for London?" Jenna asked.

"Yes, two more," I said before whispering to Gabriel, "Come on, my handsome wyvern. Let's show the vampires what dragons are made of."

Gabriel made a formal bow to Christian and Allie, then, with nods at the polters, walked forward with me.

"Thanks so much for everything," I said, pausing at the edge of the portal. The energy of it made the fine hairs on my arm stand on end. "If I had to be stuck in an airport with anyone, I'm glad it was with you all. Minus Stella, of course."

Allie and Karma said their goodbyes, and without any further delay, I stepped into the portal, Gabriel on my heels.

EPILOGUE
PARTNERS-OF-BADASSES
GROUP CHAT

From: Aisling

OK, I think I've added everyone into the chat group, all the mates and our new friends. Welcome, everyone! Also, I'd like to thank Ysolde for coming up with the name.

From: Ysolde

My pleasure. Happy New Year, everyone!

From: Allie

Hello to my fellow partners of badassery from the wilds of the Czech Republic. What a great thought to keep in touch this way. Kind of a dragon-vampire-polter meeting of minds, eh?

From: May

It is indeed an excellent think tank. And welcome, everyone. As Aisling may have mentioned, we have a Mates Union group that has been very supportive, so we thought that broadening our scope would be beneficial to everyone. Maybe we could plan on a quarterly get-together?

From: Thaisa

Hello to the new people, and thank the goddess now Phyllida and I aren't the new kids on the block anymore. My dragon is Archer. He's a storm dragon, and is seriously badass.

From: Karma

Hi everyone! Thanks for including me, and yes, I would love a quarterly shindig. I feel like after what we all went through together, we should stay in contact. Speaking of that, has there been any fallout regarding Stella?

From: Aisling

Oh, yes. Some of the blue dragons heard of her roaming around the Pacific Northwest. The information is being spread to the pertinent dragons there, so they can look for her. Regardless, all the septs are now wary of anyone outside of the dragonkin.

From: Ysolde

And a whole lot of them *in* the kin, but that's neither here nor there.

From: Phyllida

New Year's greetings, everyone, and yes, the Song Tribe ... formerly blue dragons, for the new folks ... are on the track of this Stella woman. No word yet, but Bastian—that's my particular dragon, for those who are new—Bastian is confident we'll find her.

From: Ysolde

Blue dragons are the best trackers. So, how did Christmas go for everyone? We were only home about six hours before Pavel and Holland's baby was born.

From: Aisling

How are baby Elea and Holland's sister? I just sent off packages for both.

From: Ysolde

Elea is adorable and, of course, being spoiled within

an inch of her life.

Even Baltic has admitted that as babies go, she is particularly charming. Mind you, he's delighted that the light dragons have grown by another member, but I defy anyone to think Elea isn't cute as a button. Holland's sister Amaranthe is recovering far more quickly than I ever did, and has returned home to her own children.

From: May

I'm so glad that both birth mother and baby are thriving. We just sent a few things, as well, so hopefully Pavel and Holland will get them soon. Oh, speaking of that, Maata and Tipene would like to pass along their congratulations to Pavel. I told them to just message him, but evidently that breaches some sort of dragon guard etiquette wherein they must maintain the most formal of relations, so there we are.

From: Bee

Dragons are weird, yo.

From: Bee

Also, hello to the new folks. I'm Bee, have a dragon named Constantine, and a baby on the way in about three weeks. My sister is Aoife, who is Kostya's mate, and our brother is Rowan, the red dragon wyvern. His mate is Sophea.

From: Aoife

Hi guys. Yes, Kostya is mine, and I'd like to apologize for whatever he did to piss off anyone during the blizzard. He says everyone picked on him, and that usually means he got a bit hand-wavey, so I figured I'd get the apology over with now.

Although really, whoever broke his collarbone—again—was just mean. You guys know he has a weak collarbone!

From: Ysolde
And that's exactly why each wyvern goes directly for it first thing.
From: Sophea
Hi from me, as well! We're so sorry about the blizzard that hit right as everyone was leaving our house. Rowan felt terrible. The roads were impassable, so we couldn't go rescue everyone as he wanted. We both felt terrible about the storm hitting when it did.

Also, congrats to Pavel and Holland. I didn't realize the other septs sent baby presents, but I'll take any reason to buy cute baby things that don't have to pass Constantine's scrutiny.
From: Bee
He picked the absolute worst time to go carbon neutral and insist on only organic baby things. He's even threatening to become vegan. I put my foot down at that. I don't mind forgoing most meat, but I'll be damned if I give up cheese.
From: Aoife
Dear goddess. No cheese? Is life even worth living without smoked Gouda?
From: Bee
Right?
From: Karma
Or a really sharp white cheddar. The local university's agriculture program makes a white cheddar that is almost orgasmic. Pixie has fallen in love with it, and is using it in every dish she can. I am not complaining in the least.
From: Aisling
And now I'm hungry.
From: Bee
Dammit, me too.

From: Aisling
Speaking of Pixie, how … er … man, this is awkward to ask. How are things going with any long-distance relationships she may or may not have?
From: Karma
Sigh.
From: Aisling
That well?
From: Ysolde

It can't possibly be as bad as what's going on in my house. I thought I'd survived Brom's moody teen years, but now he's storming around breathing fire everywhere, hormones flying hither and yon, doors slamming, and dramatic speeches about how much stress he's under.

In other words, we have a marvelous contradiction of a young man embracing his adulthood mingled with a teen who is having Romantic Feelings for the first time.
From: Karma

Does he write poetry? Pixie has taken to writing long poems about living alone, being alone, wandering the forest alone, and one particularly epic ditty concerning living in a house full of imps while still feeling completely and utterly alone.
From: Aisling

I sense a theme. I also am now dreading the twins hitting puberty.
From: May

Maybe dragons are easier than mortals when they get to that point?
From: Aisling
HA HA HA HA HA HA.
From: Aisling
Not according to Drake.

From: Ysolde

I just asked Baltic. He stared at me, shook his head, and said he planned on being elsewhere when Anduin was aged thirteen to eighteen. I asked if I could come with him. He said I could. #wyvernslovethebest

From: May

Gabriel's nieces are nice, and they're fourteen, seventeen, and twenty.

From: Ysolde

That's because they're on their best behavior when they visit you guys.

From: Karma

I don't know. Pixie is Pixie no matter what company she's in.

From: Aisling

I suspect Pixie is unique unto herself.

From: Karma

I think you're dead-on there. Regardless, to answer the original question, there has been much texting and video chatting going on at our end. Some days the chats go well, and Pixie is almost cheerful, and cooks up a storm. Other days, things aren't so positive, and those are the days she recites her poems to the imps. Normal house imps, mind you, not the horrible northern ones. My imps are good, if a bit dramatic at times. But I digress.

From: Aisling

Remind me to never bring Jim to your house—it has a taste for imps. How are things in the CR, Allie?

From: Allie

Well and fine, although I do have something I wanted to mention, but I was enjoying—and like Aisling, dreading the upcoming teen years of my own kids—all the Pixie/Brom drama. We got home in time for the

Christmas Eve festivities, so all was well there. Finch went off to his home in New York City, and we just got a cryptic message from him that he's disappearing for a few months, but we're not to worry. And no, before anyone asks, I have no idea what that means.

From: Aisling

Hmm. I don't feel like I know vamps well enough to speculate other than the obvious: a woman.

From: May

I second the girlfriend idea. He's very handsome, and wicked with a sword. What woman wouldn't be swayed by that?

From: Allie

I agree, but I realize that dark, brooding, sexy, and able to lop off the heads of Great Northern Imps with panache may not be every woman's dream man. Christian isn't sure what's up, and Finch won't tell him, which isn't like him at all. We'll just have to wait and see what shakes down. Oh, and what I wanted to tell you was that I asked Christian about the four king vampires, and he said they weren't kings, but thanes. I thought they were the same thing, but he said no, thanes were powerful beings originally called wealden, but after the people they tried to save turned them over to the princes of Abaddon, their sins were bound to them, and they became thanes. They were more or less demigods, however, so I guess you were right all along in that both the creators of vamps and dragons were at least some form of god.

From: May

That's fascinating. Who knew they were so similar?

From: Ysolde

Pardon me while I snort. I just hope no vamp has to suffer the way Baltic and I do.

From: Charity

Excuse me?

From: Ysolde

…

From: Ysolde

Oh hi, Charity. Fancy seeing you here.

From: Charity

It sounds like I missed some sort of a gathering. If I'm not wanted, of course I will drop the group.

From: Ysolde

No, no, you're a mate, and we added all the mates into the discussion. And yes, you missed a big kerfuffle, but it's nothing that you would have liked to attend. We were all snowed in at the same airport for several hours, during which time Aisling kept cursing us.

From: Aisling

I did not!

From: Ysolde

Well, it *seemed* like you did.

From: Aisling

All I did was try to be cheerful in the face of adversity.

From: May

Yes, but every time you did, things happened. *Bad* things.

From: Aisling

Unfortunately, I can't deny that. It wasn't the greatest experience, Charity. Except for meeting Allie and Karma and their respective families, that is.

From: Aisling

Also, yes, you are supposed to be here. We thought all the mates would like to meet our new friends. Charity is the mate of the First Dragon, ladies. They found each other a few years ago.

From: Ysolde

Why do I feel like everyone is looking at me?

From: May

Well, we kind of are, LOL.

From: Ysolde

Sigh.

From: Charity

Gotcha. I thought perhaps I had been *accidentally* left off a gathering notice because of some bad feelings by certain mates, but I'm glad to hear that's not the case.

From: Ysolde

Look, if your son had been hounded for years, for YEARS, about becoming a dragon by a freakin' demigod who SHOULD have better things to do with his time than pester a child, I'm willing to bet you would feel the same way.

From: Charity

I thought Brom wanted to become a dragon?

From: Ysolde

He did. It's just that the First Dragon put what I feel is undue pressure upon him while he was deciding.

From: Charity

Really? That's the stand you're going to make?

From: Ysolde

It's a righteous stand.

From: Charity

Who wouldn't want to be a dragon if they could?

From: Ysolde

I don't deny that, but Brom was pressured. Unduly.

From: Charity

If you really believe that, then I'll ask the First Dragon to remove the dragonhood.

From: Ysolde

...

From: Ysolde

Dammit. I hate it when I'm forced into a corner. I suppose since Brom made the decision, I will let go of my annoyance with the FD for his role in that decision being made.

From: Charity

I think life will be a lot happier for you if you do that. Sorry, did we just derail the conversation?

From: Allie

Yes, but it's a fascinating insight into what it is like to be a dragon.

From: May

Was there anything else you had to report from the vamp world, Allie? I take notes, which I will hand out to those members who miss the chat.

From: Bee

Please send me a copy of the chat. Constantine is insisting I take a nap now, and Gary has promised he'll read me a chapter of his memoirs.

From: Allie

Gary?

From: Ysolde

Gary is Bee and Constantine's disembodied head. He's very sweet, and puts on a hell of a wedding.

From: Allie

Um …

From: May

Gary kind of takes a bit of getting used to, but he's very cheerful, and loves Jim.

From: Allie

Gotcha. Let me see. … I didn't know we were doing actual reports. That's a good idea, though. So broadening. Um … not really. Christian has the members of the Moravian Society busy trying to find men who were harming vampires, but their organization—the baddies, not the vamps—seems to have crumbled, and the head honcho has disappeared. There was a blip earlier with a worrisome guy who shouldn't have been alive but was, but that's taken care of now.

From: Aisling
The thane guys?
From: Allie
No, this was only distantly related to the four big guys. It's a bit confusing, to be honest. The thralls were a descendant of the thanes. I think. Dammit, now I'll have to go look in Christian's Giant Book o' Vampy History to make sure. He only told me about the thane part.
From: May
Wow. And I thought the dragonkin had an exciting backstory.
From: Aisling
Seriously. I look forward to hearing more of the vampire lore, Allie, and do tell us if there's something you need help with in regard to the baddies.
From: May
Karma? Did you want to add anything from the polter side of things?
From: Karma
All I know is that Nephthys formed the race of polters, and I don't think it was particularly dramatic, although she was a goddess, married to the Egyptian god Seth. Other than that, everything is copacetic, polter-wise.

I do work for the Akashic League as needed, Pixie is getting therapy, and going to a local Otherworld school so the glamours don't rot her brain (as my father claims they will do), and Adam is spending more time working for the Watch than he does his mundane job with the US Marshals. That's us in a nutshell, I think.

From: Holland

Hi everyone! Sorry to pop in and dash, but we're going to give Elea a bath, and Pavel is terrified he's going to drop her, so I have to supervise. But I wanted to say hello, thank you all for welcoming me to the mates and extras group, and more thank-yous for all the kind messages about our daughter. We're thrilled to bits, and Pavel and I couldn't be prouder. Or more terrified, LOL!

From: Aisling

You'll be fine. I'm sure Ysolde is there to lend a helping hand.

From: Ysolde

I am, indeed.

From: Charity

The First Dragon intends on stopping by to visit his newest descendant soon, too.

From: Ysolde

Oh, joy.

From: Charity

Hmm?

From: Ysolde

Change-of-subject time. I believe we have a Mates Union meeting next month, but what if we shoot for a Badasses meeting in March or April?

From: May

I'll submit that suggestion of a date to everyone for thoughts, if you like.

From: Aisling

Sounds good to me. Right, I'm off to go see the half inch of snow that has hit London. The kids want to make a snowman. You can, I'm sure, picture the expression I'm wearing. Oh, Jim sends its love to everyone. It's going to Paris tomorrow to spend the weekend with its girlfriend, Cecile.

From: Allie

Do I want to know what sort of woman dates a demon in dog form?

From: May

Cecile is a Welsh corgi. A very old one. But Jim is madly in love with her, and she puts up with it, so all is well.

From: Aisling

I will officially call this meeting of the Partners of Badasses closed, then. No, Jim, you can't join the group. You're not a mate. Besides, you'd just fill it with chat about your package, and no one needs that in their life. I swear to god I'm going to get you a pair of underpants if you don't stop rolling onto your back while asking for belly scritches. Do you have any idea how embarrassing that is? What? Of course I turned off voice to text. I do *not* have a history of forgetting about it. I am the most technologically advanced person I … *merde*. It is on. Dammit, Jim, why didn't you warn me earlier, before I mentioned getting you underpants?

From: Ysolde

I'll send you a six-pack. I could go my whole life without ever seeing Jim's business again.

From: May

Amen to that.

NOTE TO READERS

My lovely one! I hope you enjoyed reading this book, which I handcrafted from the finest artisanal words just for you. If you are one of the folks who likes to review books, I'd love it if you posted a review for it on your favorite book spot (be sure to tell me if you do, so that I can lavish praise all over you).

If you're looking for some fun behind-the-scenes tidbits and exclusive material—including the PERILS OF EFFRI-JIM short story, which is available free just for you via Book-funnel—hie thee over to my website at katiemacalister.com and sign up for the newsletter.

ABOUT THE AUTHOR

For as long as she can remember, Katie MacAlister has loved reading. Growing up in a family where a weekly visit to the library was a given, Katie spent much of her time with her nose buried in a book.

Two years after she started writing novels, Katie sold her first romance, *Noble Intentions*. More than seventy books later, her novels have been translated into numerous languages, been recorded as audiobooks, received several awards, and have been regulars on the *New York Times, USA Today, Publishers Weekly*, and *Wall Street Journal* bestseller lists. Katie lives in the Pacific Northwest with two dogs, and can often be found lurking around online.

You are welcome to join Katie's official discussion group on Facebook, as well as connect with her via TikTok and Instagram. For more information, visit her website at www.katiemacalister.com